Dancing flames

Dancing flames

Jayanti Sahu

Invincible Publishers

Published by
Invincible Publishers
201A, SAS Tower, Sector 38, Gurugram – 122003
Phone: +91-124-4034247, +91 9355675555
www.i-publish.in

First Published in 2020

ISBN: 978-93-89600-76-6

Dedicated to all the people I've met on the course of my life; some known, some unknown and for more to come…

Acknowledgement

Certain things in life are like a vague and distant dream, which we believe are almost impossible to achieve. Yet when they do come true, I believe some people do deserve a token of gratitude and appreciation for their greater efforts to convert someone's dream into a reality.

I would like to thank Mr. Ajay and Sagar Setia for owning and managing such a wonderful publishing house. I would like to thank Ms. Divya Arora who acted as a torch bearer for the entire project, without whom none of it would have begun in the first place. I would like to thank the finest Editor-in-Chief Mrs. Chandni Mathur and my absolutely wonderful editor Ms. Akshita Sharma for adding finesse to my work. I'd like to express my heartfelt gratitude to my illustrator Ms. Shrishti Prabhakar for her fantastic work on the cover page. I'd also like to thank Mr. Kumara Gurubaran for managing the finance regarding the publication. I'd like to thank the entire team of Invincible Publishers for being a part of my world in this and for helping me out.

I'd like to thank my mom for all those endless supplies of Chandamama and the heaps of children's magazines which kindled the interest of writing in me. I'd like to thank my dad for encouraging me to chase my dreams and for being there in every way I could possibly imagine. I'd like to thank my friends and online writing pals whom I've never met till now, yet who have managed to encourage me and by reviewing my work. Technology is indeed a blessing.

The amount of gratitude that I feel towards these people is so heartfelt and intense that it is quite impossible to express it but feel it in my heart. Kudos to the team and everyone involved in this!

Preface

Greetings to my dearest reader!

I wrote this novel when I dropped out of school in 2018 as an 11th grade science student because I wasn't good enough for it, for my heart lay within the pages of literary endeavours. It took around five months for me to complete this before I rejoined school again and honestly, I never regretted it. It gave me ample amount of time to swim into the deepest depths of the oceans of my wild and crazy imagination and voila! here it is.

I'd like to say that life is a concoction of various tastes. At times it could be sweet, at times savoury, at times they will be too bitter. There might be bland days ahead as well. But what gives meaning to relationships and our connection with people around is how much we value them and the efforts that we put into it to make them work. It is our values, morals and our principles which keep us going forward.

Love is an important aspect of life which plays a vital role in binding us together. And to truly experience it is a blessing indeed. Love is so powerful that it makes things and destroys things as well. Amidst all those that love does, this is just a simple attempt to exhibit the positive side of love, how love guides us and how love mends people and changes the bad ones into better people.

Love is not only about feeling the butterflies in your stomach or feathers along your spine. It's the unconditional aspect of it, the courage to accept the other person the way they are and most importantly to sacrifice which matters. It's not about having expectations but to rise above them all. Love is all about walking on a path of thorns, bleeding and hurting, yet smiling because their presence just makes everything so painless and bearable. And at the end of the day there are many of us who will relate to the fact that,

"It's hard for me to love, but when I do, I love a little too hard…"

Jayanti Sahu (Author)
Rourkela, 2020

Contents

Drowning

It was difficult for me to comprehend that I had grown into a big girl. It's funny yet unacceptable to see the fleeting childhood fly away to a place you can never retrieve it back from. I stared at myself in the mirror for a good five minutes. My jet black hair sat like a messy mop at the top of my head, its edges squarely framing my face. My eyes had become bloodshot and puffy, my face bloated. I sighed as I splashed some water on my face and went back staring at myself. I hardly slept properly at night anymore. Mom had already started sending me off to various tutors even before the school started. She wanted me to get into some good college; IIT, NIT, AIIMS or JIPMER, maybe?

"You can't do this…"

"This is far beyond your reach…"

"UGH! This is frustrating!"

"What if I didn't want to do it in the first place?"

"Asha! How much more time will you take to get ready? It's already 7: 40! Get ready fast or you'll get late for class!"

I sighed.

"Coming, Ma!" I strained out a yell. I didn't want to go back to that horrid place once again. But I had to. I had no choice, had I?

I slipped on a T-shirt and slid my legs into a pair of jeans, grabbed my books and hurriedly dumped them into a backpack. I slung it around my arm and made my way to the living room.

Mom caressed my face, causing me to flinch as her cold hands touched my warm, feverish skin.

"Aww, my *bachcha* is studying so hard nowadays. I'll have your favourite *chana masala* made by the time you come back home from the classes." She said smiling.

There was no warmth in it. Or maybe I didn't receive any.

And, *chana masala* wasn't even my favourite…

I faked a smile. She was about to say something again but her words were interrupted by the annoying honking of the auto horn.

"Coming!" My mom yelled out as I slid in my chappals and made my way to the vehicle. I sat on the cold seat ready to go. I looked out to see my mom waving her hand with a big smile on her face. I waved my hand back to her, whispering a small "Bye" , as the vehicle started.

The vehicle jerked as it started, gaining its speed.

Earlier, I didn't even have to tell her anything and she would guess. I would come home minding my own business when she would approach me and ask me about what went wrong before I let it all out to her. But now, even if I dropped hints at some time or the other, mom didn't seem to notice. Or maybe she did. I would never know.

I looked out, the wind hitting my face allowing my eyes to swallow back my tears, as the auto tottered away on the damaged and broken road.

The Hunt

We saw her walking into the building. We have had been following her for the past month. It seemed like she moved around in the same locality for taking her classes.

Monday: 6-7:30

Tuesday: 5-6:30

And on the rest days of the week: 7-8:30

We couldn't operate at her school, there were too many people. We couldn't afford to get noticed or grab much attention, so this was the only time we could work besides mornings or afternoons.

We waited there for about an hour and a half. We saw her getting out with a bunch of students and waiting at the far end of the street. She waited for about seven minutes before her regular driver came and picked her up from the spot.

I flipped open my cell phone and dialed,

"*Da, skazki,*" said the voice at the other end.

"Location of the target is specified. We need to act."

"I'll send you the directions in two days, till then wait and don't attract much attention. Stay in your hideout till the further message is conveyed."

"*Ladno,*" I said before hanging up on him.

The night after, one of us was lying down at the backseat while the other was on vigil.

"Wake up! There's somebody here!" He whispered to me.

My eyes shot open. We couldn't afford anybody finding out about our secret hideout. I pulled out my gun and kept it ready at bay.

I pulled out my thermal camera and pointed it out in the direction we had heard the footsteps. No wonder, we were all nervous and scared. I saw a young girl checking out her phone.

"Just a lass, chill," I said to my counterpart.

"Be careful though," He said.

"Hmm..." I said switching it off.

I had drifted off for a few seconds but then I woke up again. There was something unsettling about that girl. All the neurons in my brain shot up with energy as I realized the uncanny similarities between our target and the girl.

I sat up again.

"What happened?" He asked.

"We might have the deer walked up to the lion's den itself."

"Huh?" He asked confused.

I rummaged through our devices' bag and pulled out the night vision camera and turned it on. A wicked smile crept on my lips as I realized that it was indeed her.

"Oh, that's her."

He looked up at me.

"What is she doing here? In a place like this, and that too at this hour?"

"Not our problem, *slaboumny*," I replied. "I wonder if we should kidnap her now."

"We haven't received the orders yet."

"But we might get a raise. This seems like a good chance."

"But what if she has a police troop with her?"

He had a point but waiting and letting go of such a good opportunity would have been a waste. So I went out of my den to explore a bit.

I came back home tired and mentally worn out; the smell of *chana masala* was wafting into my nostrils, exciting my nasal sensors.

My head was filled with a little excitement and a little worry. My heart was beating hard inside my chest. I had spent the entire chemistry class planning on how I would break my decision to my mom. It was now or never.

"Ma! I'm back!" I yelled.

"Wash your hands and feet. Dinner's ready," she said.

We were sitting at the dining table, eating food when I blurted out, "Ma, I don't like science, I want to take up Humanities."

She glared at me for a while.

I knew it should have been me taking hold of my life and making my own decisions. But as every typical Indian boy or girl, I had to ask my parents if I could take up humanities as my majors in high school. I got a nice slap across my face and a two-hour long rant stating how useless humanities was and how I would not get a good job if I took up that for higher studies in future. After all that went on, I was made to grasp one thing, 'No humanities.'

My parents had my admission done in a school where my ex-boyfriend had studied. I thought I'd meet him and the girl again; our mutual friend who had once got us together. But what I had heard from the students felt like a knife stabbed straight at my heart.

I could not believe that our friend had actually biased him into thinking that I had found someone new and that I had been in a relationship with that person when all I had asked her to convey was that I cared for him and that his education was more important than what we had, which could be saved up for later.

I still loved him from all my heart. I thought that maybe after a prosperous future, he would come after me and thank me for at least that my decision was right. The fact that someone I had loved earlier and still did; thought wrong and horribly of me was unbearable.

He would never have thanked me. People were too selfish anyway. Why would he come back to someone like me after growing into someone successful? But the fact that what I did was right consoled me, or maybe that was what I thought.

I was surprised at how boldly I had swallowed the news myself. But then I could do nothing because he and his girlfriend, both, had moved out of town to a conventional school to study and be together.

I sighed and went on to do my work. I was glad that I hardly knew anybody at that school, so I was on my own most of the times. Things started tensing up during lessons. My parents had enrolled me up for six extra classes other than my school. I used to be tired and hardly got any time for writing anything.

I could not feel myself fitting into that scientific atmosphere. Every second felt suffocating, as if creating a conflict between me and my life. Writing stories and reading English books had become my sanctuary...but little did anyone at home understand.

I did poorly in my exams, and another humiliation coming my way in front of so many unknown students, and teachers was overwhelming. So I started making excuses and staying back at home again. I would say that I was unwell or that there were fewer classes and that the teachers used to be absent which was somewhat true. A public sector industrial organization ran the school, and they hired most of the teachers on a contractual basis.

The school was perfect for students who wanted to appear for the nationwide entrance examinations for engineering or medical schools, which required much more extra information than that of the school and board prescribed syllabus. And I was forced to do the same; preparing to appear for such exams. I used to stay back at home to read, but instead of that, I used to open my writing website for reading and writing and talking to my friends who lived abroad, who meant the world to me and whom I was planning to meet at some or the other course of my life. And that was when I met a guy named Daniel Thompson.

Daniel and I hit it off really soon and really well. It was love at first text. I used to mess about in role play with him a lot. He asked me if I had Instagram and I refused since I did not have one and I was forbidden as my parents were over-aware of cybercrime.

Staying within so many limitations used to irritate me. I was afraid that Daniel would leave me. But he was sweet, caring and understanding.

He had everything I looked for in a guy. We loved each other to death. I trusted him more than anything else and did not hesitate to share my life with him and all that I had gone through. He was very supportive. Despite living in another continent, he did everything that even the people closest to me could not. He strived to learn and understand me, and for the first time, I felt I was worth something and that I meant something to someone. I knew we had to meet up, but I was scared of losing him. He knew of my insecurities and always used to promise and console me that he would come and visit me and that we would have something together.

We looked forward to the future, getting our dream jobs, loving each other eternally, marrying, having kids, watching them grow and getting old together and die to reincarnate and start our lovely journey as strangers all over again. We were determined to break the myth that online relationships never worked. But as usual, my happy days did not last for long.

I stayed at home for two months without attending school.

Daniel and I used to chat every second of the day. We used to spend sleepless nights talking to each other. The spark of excitement between us was infinite, and we wanted to stay like that forever.

After two months and a few days, the school called my mom up, asking what was the reason that I was not attending school anymore and if I had left for somewhere else. I remember mom coming home from work in rage and anger. I received all the hate in the world from her that day in the form of cuts, scratches, bruise, and a black eye.

They informed mom that I had failed in three subjects out of five, I had to study a lot more and had barely managed to pass in the other two. The next day I remember sitting in the principal's office waiting for him to come into the room. My mom was sitting beside me in another chair.

My heart was racing. For a Mary Sue that I was from the beginning, this was a huge turning point in my life. I was staring at my hands trying not to think about the past. I was trying to be bold, but I knew I was failing miserably at this. I was scared of what the Principal would say even if I willingly wanted to be expelled so that I could start over and take up humanities.

I was looking outside the window, at the fluttering butterflies, the chirping birds and the still trees whose leaves gently swayed in the warm afternoon breeze. I was wondering how happy they might be out there, flying away to wherever they wanted, high to the clouds, running over the towns, to the trees and where not. If I had wings, I would have flown far away, far-far away from the people around me, far away to a beautiful montane forest surrounded by birds and animals and trees, just like a perfect angel residing in her natural sanctuary.

Or I would have flown miles away to Daniel, living the ideal life we had imagined for ourselves. I came out of my thoughts by the broaching sound of the creaking door. I was too scared to look up, the sound of the footsteps echoing in the room magnified in my ears. I saw him walking to the big leather office chair and taking his seat. There was a look of annoyance on his face. There was a thing in his hands that scared me the most, my report card. I saw a peon walking into the room with a thick record book in his hands. He placed it on his table and walked out.

"Hmmm..." was all that he said putting on his glasses and opening my report card and the record book.

I was trembling like a leaf under the impact of the harsh winter wind. I felt oddly cold even though the windows were open, the garish afternoon's sun rays trying to singe me, my thoughts traveling back to my days as a kid under the banyan tree with my uncle.

I wish I could go back to that time somehow by magic. I wanted the ground to swallow me.

I was struggling hard to hold back my tears and saw my mother looking at me with big red eyes.

"So.....you're Asha Mohini? Hm?" He asked with a dead serious voice.

"Yes sir," I said trying my best to maintain my composure.

"You've been absent from your classes for the last two months, any specific reason you have got to defend yourself?"

"Yes, sir. I was absent for about two months since I was unwell and sick," I said making this pathetic excuse.

"May I see your medical reports?"

"I haven't gotten any. I was resting at my home until I felt better."

"What kind of disease takes two whole months to get cured without any medication from a practicing doctor? Do you think you can get away lying like this?" He stood up from his chair banging hard on his desk which startled me.

I knew principals were strict, but I had never been dealt with this harshly by an outsider before.

I looked down at my fingers which lay on my lap, saying nothing.

"Why are you speechless now? And what kind of score is this? And you say to your parents we don't teach at school? Huh?"

He said in his booming voice slapping the report card on the desk in front of me.

Mom must have told him of my excuses. I wanted to glare at mom. There was a heavy tension in the air.

I was close to having a meltdown. I might have failed horribly, but I knew the teachers never taught anything in class. The teachers were often absent. I could not argue with him since I was on the inferior side right now.

I remember coming home from school after that disastrous event. Dad said a lot of hurtful things over the phone in front of my mom, and I had to listen to every word they had to say. He kept on praising his nephew, on how good he was at everything.

My mind traveled back to the day when I was younger. He had brought a small bag full of coins from various countries of the world. I had extended my arms thinking they were for me, but he had asked me not to touch them since those were for Shyam *bhaiya*, my cousin.

He would bring expensive gifts for him and would come home bringing cheap chocolates for me. I was a kid who easily got jealous, and this attitude of his made me think that he did not love me. I knew he was born before I was and my dad who was unmarried by then doted on him as his own son.

I did not have a problem if he loved him more than he loved me but what hurt me the most that I was being compared, being made to feel low and deplorable of myself and the fact of my failing in the subjects. It was understandable when mom did it, but dad doing it for the first time, hurt me a lot. I thought he was a better man and that he understood me a lot more than mom did, but I was wrong. After hanging up, my mom hit the back of my head with her purse.

That day was horrible. I could not face mom or anybody for the matter. Everyone in school knew what had happened. I bet I was the subject of discussion everywhere, the bad example about which every mommy warns her child. I knew that it was a terrible conduct, but there was a long history of dark reasons, and I did not expect anybody to understand either.

I knew people loved to say things and bitch about other people without giving second thoughts to it but I never really cared because I knew I was right. I lived in a small town. It was not difficult for words to spread. In fact, the hearsay would spread like wildfire in any dry forest of California. I got out of the vehicle and started making my way to the classroom building when all I felt was weary as I was not up for another humiliating session, especially by a group. I bunked my class that evening and started making my way to an isolated bridge which was at about a twenty or twenty-five-minute walking distance from where I came for tuitions.

I put my hood on and left my bag at some random place and started walking. My paternal family house was on the way, so I had to be careful. I was thankful that it was already dark. I was walking down the road. There were a few motorcycles and bicycles that went past me, but I kept walking with my hands inside my pocket. I was mentally praying that no one noticed me. My mom was a senior executive officer in an industrial firm which belonged to the government. My dad too was a government official and very socially active so almost everyone in town knew my parents and me and therefore, I was too scared to be caught. I saw a few shops on my way. Some sold electronics while some were stationery shops.

There were even a few shops selling hot snacks. The smell of deep-fried samosas wafted into my nose making my mouth water. I had some money, but I could not risk being caught. So I kept walking till I reached the most isolated part of the town which lay at one end of the civilization. It was pitch dark there. The light of the street lamps did not reach to the bridge, and the water of the river down looked like a flowing stream of tar.

People in the town liked narrating and embedding fear into others' minds by narrating scary stories about the bridge, often claiming to have experienced something supernatural and dark there. It was all up to people to believe if things like that existed. For example, mom thought that those stories were faulty and false because as a kid, every time, she would cross the cremating grounds to go to her uncle's house in another village all alone and never experienced anything spooky whereas I liked to accept their existence.

If humans can exist, why can't they?

It all depends on people, what they've gone through and their experiences which lead them to believe what they want or what they don't. Returning to the scary legends of the bridge, some said there was a ghost of a young girl who was sexually exploited and murdered brutally by a group of men, and that she would push the person to the water down the bridge if anyone dared to lean against the bridge to look down at the water below. Some told silly stories about some demon, who was invoked on the viaduct by a group of witches and was still lurking around as he never got a chance to go back to hell.

But unfortunately for them, the darkness did scare me a bit but not at that moment; I wanted to be in the dark and isolation to let some of those unwanted events go. And I would have been glad to keep the sad ghostly girl or the poor stuck up demon some company, not minding how crazy that sounds.

I was staring down at the water below which looked black in the darkness of the night with the moon shining on the sky, her round reflection falling on the water. Maybe she was looking down to earth at Endymion as he was asleep somewhere in a cave in Greece, on Mount Latmus.

I smiled a little at how silly my thoughts were. I sighed as I felt my head going a bit heavy and my body a bit tired and sore from the bruises that I had after a severe beating that afternoon. I adjusted my glasses looking at the barely visible horizon ahead of me. All I could see were tall trees which seemed still as a series of statues.

I kept staring at the scene around me and all of a sudden I felt the urge to let it all out. All the horrible memories came flooding to me like a helpless creature amidst a raging sea.

It had been a long time since I had cried out of any emotions and this was such moment. I scratched the metal railing of the bridge with my fingertips sobbing out loudly. I wanted Mother Nature to know what a cursed life she had bestowed upon me. I was failing in life, in my career and in everything that had mattered more than anything else to me. I wondered how amazing it would have been if someone was there just rubbing my back and whispering soothing and encouraging words into my ears, but I knew I was far away from what I had imagined my life would be like.

I huddled myself close to prevent the cold night air to get to me. There was a strange vibe in the air that night. Something told me that things would change. It was comforting, but I felt as if it was too good to come true.

My head was reeling in all the confusing thoughts. I felt my phone vibrate and took out my phone to take a look at it. I had a notification from the app where Daniel and I used to talk. I opened it to see that I had got a text from Daniel. I looked at it smiling. No matter how sad I would be, a text from him always made me beam with delight. I glanced at the time at the top right of my screen realizing that I had thirty-five minutes left. I started to walk from the center to the end of the bridge, the same way I had entered when I heard heavy thuds behind me in the darkness.

Surely, the bridge was made when British ruled India about a hundred years ago. And it was past its expiry date. No one used that bridge because there was another one-two kilometers down from which I was standing on, which was actually meant to be used, well furnished with lighting.

Is the bridge cracking? Is the ghost rumor veracious? Why does it sound like footsteps?

There were millions of reasons running in mind to what that sound was, some being absolutely impossible and delusional. I just turned around when I felt two huge arms tackle my body squeezing me tight, almost suffocating me. I was panicking. I felt all the air being compressed and sucked out of my lungs.

I tried to kick his crotch and hit him with my elbows, but none worked. He was holding onto me too tightly.

"Ah...tsk tsk......a feisty kitty now, aren't you?" The man chuckled into my ears.

I could not scream or cry since my mouth was muffled hard with large hands and I was held tight by beefy arms of some stranger who towered over me like a giant. He smelled like an unaltered pile of moth-eaten newspapers, musky and woodsy, mixed with a tint of raw flesh and blood. I wanted to throw up and at the same time, I was sobbing hard from the pain that emanated from my skull out of his tight grip on my hair. I felt him snatching my phone away from my hands and tossing it out into the water down below. I could see that Daniel had sent something, a picture of him, or his kittens maybe...or maybe a meme to make me laugh or just a romantic gif speaking his heart out.

I wanted to run away from his grasp to get my phone, but I was helpless. Hot tears were streaming down my face and the next thing I knew was a stinging pain of a needle piercing through the skin of my arm, and I saw the curtains of consciousness closing up on me.

I found my head resting on someone's lap when I woke up. I had not opened my eyes fully yet, even if I wanted to. I did not know what kept holding me back from doing such a simple thing, but for some reason, it just did not feel right.

I could feel as if I was in a congested place. Even my legs were in someone else's lap, and the mid part of my body felt oddly low. I felt like a bent bow. The person on whose lap I was resting my head on was holding my left arm to prevent me from falling on the base of the vehicle we were in. I could feel his hold let go of me when I woke up from unconsciousness.

"I know you're awake," the man said with a thick Russian accent. At first, it was confusing for me if it was Russian or French.

I yelped and clutched onto his leather jacket when the vehicle received a bump, squeezing my eyes shut.

"You can open your eyes," the same man said.

I fluttered open my eyelids, squeezing them shut again as the harsh artificial light from the street lamps along the road on which we were moving on, came through the un-tinted windows of the van and hit my sensitive balls of vision. It was still night. It took me a while to get adjusted to my surroundings. He let me sit up, and I finally settled myself between the strangers.

I clutched my head tight, almost ripping out my hair from the headache and frustration. All that happened; the incident at the bridge, the kidnapping and everything came flooding back to me. I was crazy enough to be happy that I had gotten away from my family, but I started freaking out about losing Daniel.

A bit of bad always comes with the good whereas a bit of good comes along with the bad.

"Umm...can I get your phone, please? I desperately need to talk to my boyfriend and check up on him. He lives in the United States. I promise no one will know about our whereabouts." I tried negotiating with the man.

"What makes you think that we would even care about what relations you have?" He said in a lifeless voice not turning his head elsewhere but constantly looking at the windscreen in front of us. I was getting frustrated and restless. I needed to talk to Daniel, and I was getting insane because I was being kept devoid of it.

He used to get offended over silliest things. The fact that I had not replied to his texts while going offline suddenly might have pissed him off. I knew I had grown addicted to him. He was the medicine I had become used to, to keep my mental state sound and maintained. The fact that I could not talk to him frustrated me more than the fact that I was not willing to do so.

I was in rage and anger. I knew I was sitting calm and composed, but then there were multiple nuclear explosions going on inside my head. In the smoothest and the most unexpected moment, I forcefully tried to open the vehicle door when the two men tried pulling me back inside. I bit one of the guy's hand as hard as I could earning a groan from him while the driver looked back in concern. I tried shaking the driver vigorously so that he may stop the car and that was when one of them yanked my hair and pressed a cloth to my nose which came to me unexpected. I smelled something faint like some spirit and felt my body growing limp while black dots covered my vision.

"She is savage," was all I heard before falling into the pair of arms again.

I guess I woke up again a lot later than I was expecting to. I opened my eyes to find nothing. Everything was dark and invisible. It reminded me of the atmosphere back at home when there used to be power cuts long before we got an inverter. I would be studying or flipping through the pages of my picture book and then there would be a power cut plunging us in an unknown world of void and darkness.

I would not move or shift till I would see certain features of mom's face when she lit a candle or turned on the torch. The room I was right now in just felt like that, nostalgia hit me hard taking me back to those days. It was as if the world had fell silent for a moment and came to a standstill except for the coyotes, crickets, cicadas and the garden frogs outside who perhaps loved to break the silence, filling the surroundings with their vibrating and high pitched noises.

As a kid, I would hold on to my mother's dress from behind as she led me outside the house where we would sit on the temporary chairs on the cemented pathway enjoying the natural breeze, which was a lot better than the air we got at home from the ceiling and table fans.

Small fireflies would roam and fly all around us. It looked like a fairyland, magical and beautiful.

But there were no crickets, no cicadas and no fireflies where I was there then at that moment, not even the croaks of the garden frogs to break the silence which never failed to scare the hell out of me as a kid. There were no fireflies to make the atmosphere look mystical. I was searching for the familiar things and suddenly, I started wondering what might have had happened back at the town.

What would the people be thinking about me?

Were my parents worried about me?

Had they called the cops?

Or had they continued with their lives just as usual?

What would Daniel be thinking?

Would he be worried about me?

Or just like other jerks that I had dated online before, he would have moved on to someone new...

The idea of him falling for anyone else was unbearable enough and yet here I was abducted by total strangers.

Who are they?

What did they want from me?

Why me?

Had they been following me? For how long?

I bet they might have had been targeting for me for quite a while. No one would wait on any isolated, unlit bridge every day expecting for someone to walk into it so that they could kidnap him or her.

My mind wandered around my gallery of knowledge, thinking about the reason to why they might have kidnapped me.

Ransom was not an option. Both of my parents were government officials and made enough, but that did not mean that we were millionaires and rich enough that they would kidnap me and extract all of our financial juices and suck us dry and throw us on the road.

There was a high probability that they might have abducted me for human organ trafficking and escort business. That thought scared me. I wanted my life to change but for the better, not for the worse.

I was tied down by ropes all around me. I could not even move an inch. I desperately wanted to break free. I knew I would not be able to run away no matter how hard I tried. They were too strong and smart for me, and there was no way I could outwit them.

My head was aching badly; my stomach was growling out of hunger. I wonder for how many days I had been out for. I was a little claustrophobic. I was getting nervous each passing moment.

I felt bile rising up my throat, but I fought back the urge to throw up. I was hungry, and maybe that was why such a thing was happening. I tried sniffing myself, and I realized that I smelled like a caged zoo animal. I felt a funny taste in my mouth.

I had not brushed for a couple of days. I prayed I did not get cavities or any such oral disorders. I bet there was a horde of bacteria having a sweet little party in there. The darkness was so overbearing that for a second I doubted that they had gouged out my eyes or something, so that I could not see anything.

I was not feeling well or secure in that environment.

I hated the darkness.

It scared me.

Mother used to say that the darkness was for negative people. I yelled out and grunted squirming uncomfortably.

"Let me out, you morons! I hope you die in hell, you ugly bastards! You all will burn in the darkest pits of hell!"

I heard heavy footsteps. A loud, cranky sound of the metal door opening announced their arrival. I could see a faint speck of light entering into the dark room I was in, and the footsteps were getting louder and louder with each passing second.

I wondered what was in my system. I was hungry, yet not tired. Something didn't feel right. I felt someone coming closer to me and going behind me, his silhouette somewhat visible. I felt someone's breath fanning my neck sending chills up my spine. The sound of the ropes being cut and snapped off gave me a micro feeling of freedom. Before I could pull out my arms for stretching, the man grabbed my hands and handcuffed me.

"Don't you people even let your hostages stretch, you idiots!" I spat with pure hatred lacing my words.

I felt my hair being yanked out the third time. Tears welled up in my eyes again from the pain, but I managed to hold back a sob.

"Watch what you're talking, girl," he said.

He grabbed me by my collar and pulled me outside the room. I could hear busy roads outside, as I looked outside the window in front of me. I saw electric wires about a meter away.

That was enough to tell me that I was on the third or fourth floor of some building amidst a busy place. He stopped for a moment and looked at me with that emotionless look on his face and pulled me further down the hallways which had rooms on either side. I saw skinny women dressed in revealing sequin clothes and their face caked in makeup. They were giggling and looking at me while I was being taken past them wearing dirty denim pants and a t-shirt which said, 'Drink beer, Save water' which I found to be quite hilarious.

I looked down behind from my hazy dirty glasses in shame and humiliation.

I then passed some rooms from where I heard disgusting moans and noises coming. It was not long before I realized that I was in a bordello. I tried tugging at my cuff and shaking violently trying to get away from him. I could see where my life was going.

I did not want to end up like that. I did not know the way out, but at least I could try to figure it out before anything wrong happened to me.

But unfortunately for me, I was kept under utter secrecy and strict confinement to do so.

"What do you want from me?" I yelled irritated.

He said nothing but shoved me into a room and locked it from outside. I kept banging the door with a side of my body when I heard giggles from behind.

I turned back and saw several girls sitting there on a massive bed with a fat woman who had a *bindi* between her brows, which was as big as twice the size of my thumb. To be honest, she looked like some character straight out of a Hindi soap opera. Somewhat like a typical mother-in-law who made her daughter-in-law work all day long. She would look like a hideous version of Ursula if painted in dark lavender. A few human servers were laughing and giggling while some sat there, all quiet and shut.

They looked all prepped and ready as if they were going on a party or something. But I knew they had themselves groomed like that for men who came to do violating things to them against their will just by paying some amount of money. A woman was like a flower after all. Every woman deserved to be treated with respect and care. If not for the men like these customers, such beautiful girls would not be in a state like this. The fact that this was happening made me feel sad the amount it made me feel angry. And it was pitiful how these girls and women could not fight back and were stuck up in a place like this. They sure would have difficulty merging in with the society and the cruel world, similar to how it would have a hard time accepting them for who they were.

They say that 'Eyes are the windows to the soul.' And I could look right through them. Leaping into the murky waters of their souls, I could see the reflection of their dark past in their eyes. Some were maybe confused, giggling and laughing all the time. Perhaps they had given up and accepted the lives they were living, thinking that the situation was never going to change and that it was better to live through the torture with happiness than weeping their lives away. There were some who looked dead serious. One moment they would be smiling, the other moment perhaps they would reminisce their old memories thinking about their past happy moments even if the times had been rough.

In a corner sat a girl whose name, I found out later, was Mauni. I found out that Mauni had some vocal issues and used to stutter. But despite all of that, I could see a strange fire in her eyes. Just like fire in the tawny eyes of a tiger focused on a deer to prey on, but then there was also a hint of dullness in her eyes which kind of symbolized that she was scared and nervous.

Maybe she wanted to strike back and so did I. I could imagine us being the two tigers trying to prey on the bad people, who always but backed off due to the hostile situation. And that was when I knew that I had to befriend her.

I made a face looking at her earning a mocking smile from her.

"Asha...Asha Mohini," was all that I said.

I could hear the clinking noise of small pieces of metals coming in contact with each other and finally realized they were keys; when the fat woman pulled out a huge bunch of maybe a thousand keys from the edge of her saree from somewhere around her waist and removed the cuff from my hands.

"Mohini…hmm...you will be called that from now on."

I gave out a squeal of joy in my mind when she gestured Mauni towards me. Mauni held my index finger and led me to some other room and opened a cupboard handing me a plastic packet, the toothbrush in it clearly visible. She opened a drawer and pulled out a bottle of cheap nail polish. She took the package from my hand and pulled out the brush throwing its plastic cover in a nearby bin.

She wrote 'MH' on the brush with it so that other girls knew that it was mine. There were bunk beds all around, so I knew that I had to share the room with many other girls, and therefore, the identification of personal things was necessary. For the first time in my life, I felt open and free even if I was captivated. It was rather strange for me to why I felt that way. Or maybe, because I was getting closer to my destiny.

I smiled a bit at her and took it from her hands. She pulled out a measuring tape from the nearby dresser and measured me. For a moment, I doubted if she was merely a seamstress or one of them. I saw her making her way to the cupboard again, this time she bent down and pulled out some clothes and handed me a set of new inner garments and a black tank top and khaki shorts.

I took it from her hands and thanked her for being grateful for all that she just did. That was the nicest I had been treated in a long time, and my mind was screaming in happiness for it.

"Thank you for everything." I said with a wide grin on my face.

She smiled back at me saying, "W…welcome."

She showed me the way to the bathroom and waited outside for me to freshen up. I called her in after I was done.

She asked me to wait and gestured me to sit on the bed. I saw her going out of the room, down the hallway disappearing from the line of my sight. She returned with a tray of hot food. I ate it all till the last morsel. In fact, I was gorging on the food like a monster, taking it all down with huge swigs of water. At that moment, I could not think of table manners or proper etiquettes. I was like a hungry wolf, and I had to feed myself off, and that's all I knew. She was considerate enough not to judge me by what I was doing. She just sat beside me giving an understanding look which I was relieved and thankful for.

She told me that I was out for three days straight. I could not believe my ears.

"What? Three days? Ugh, you can't be serious!"

"N…no th…three days."

"How old are you?"

"N...nineteen."

"Oooh, for how long have you been here?"

"S...since f...five. My m...mom, s...step m...mother sold me h... here."

I felt pity for her. Getting introduced to all such things at such a young age must have been a lot more difficult for her to cope with. But I was filled with admiration and awe for this determined young girl, unfazed by her flaws and who still managed to survive her dismal life with such tolerance. But moreover, I was happy as ever that I finally had someone to call as a friend.

"Anything that you like to do?" I asked her smiling.

I saw her face lit up with an unknown delight and energy when I asked her that question.

"I...I...I like s...sewing. I...I want t...to...o...open my o...own b...boutique one d...day." She said happily.

It was courageous of her to dream this big even after being exposed to so much of negativity and hardships.

She asked the mistress if I could sleep with her that night to which she hesitated at first but agreed with some persuasion in the afternoon. I went inside her room in the evening after having snacks that she had prepared. She had a beautiful room indeed. It was strange to see her having her own space while the others had to share rooms. Later I found out that she was more or less like a daughter to the mistress and was primarily brought up there, so she had her own personal lifestyle, different than the other prostitutes who were mainly traded and kidnapped from other places.

There were posters and paper cuttings of different models wearing different kinds of dresses and lingerie all on her walls. I could see a Miranda Kerr one among all that crowd of pictures. I could remember that cutting from Victoria's Secret catalog.

There was a modern and sophisticated sewing machine and bits of fabric of different colors had been swept and collected in a neat pile in one corner of the room.

She opened her fancy almirah and showed some of her most creative works, and I could not help but stare in wonder at her creations. It was confirmed that she was loaded with talent and skill. It was difficult for me to believe that such a young girl could self-teach herself and yet make such exquisite pieces of clothing without any training.

She told me that she made dresses for girls who were meant to serve rich guys who offered a lot of money and that she knew how to make western attires which had left me gaping. She told me that she used to copy designs from renowned designers and often customize it to her own taste to make it look even better; her wardrobe was a proof of her words.

She laid down some beautiful dresses that I had managed to see only on television, on models and actresses who walked on ramps with their flair. I felt the fabric with my fingertips. I knew those were the standard fabrics that were available in any shop, unlike professional designers who preferred expensive ones with variations on texture, shade, and features I was ignorant about. But her little world mesmerized and left me in shock and wonder.

"You'd make a great designer one day." I complimented her still not able to take my eyes off the dresses.

She gave me a modest smile and kept quiet.

I had owned only one dress my entire life back at the sixth grade when my mom had forced me to buy one as she wanted me to look formal and presentable at the wedding reception of her colleague's daughter and well, that was the first and last time I ever wore one. That thing kept rotting away in the cupboard till I outgrew it and then mom had to give that away to our maid's daughter.

According to her, it was better that someone wore it instead of it being thrown away just like that. I remember mom's face, to how disappointed she was that she had to give away such an expensive and new piece of clothing. I still remember her words,

"What a shame," and a sigh following it.

She laid down some of the dresses of my size and pulled out a green one which seemed a little small for me.

"This is a d...darling," she said smiling and caressing at the folded piece of clothing, " My b...best c...creation."

She pulled out a small polythene bag and put the dress in it. I was wondering what she was about to do with it when she handed it to me saying, "A t...token f...for our n...new f...found f...friendship."

That made me tear up. I tackled her in a bear hug letting tears flow freely. She kept holding me close to her, rubbing my back slowly.

"L...let it a...all o...out," was all that she said.

"I don't want to do all these things," I said sobbing.

She made me look at her while wiping away my tears. She pulled me to a corner and whispered into my ears.

"Y...you'll not be staying h...here. I...I cannot s...say w...what w...will happen e...else t...they will kill y...you and m...me a... and the m...mistress. I...I w...wish I...I could help..." She said trailing off.

I was sobbing again. She started tearing up too. I needed someone to console me and I could not thank enough for fate to have given me such a precious friend as her at the moment. Life had become like a somber surprise that I had yet to see, with dark secrets that I yet had to unravel.

She cracked a few jokes that I had no heart to laugh at. But she managed to make me smile at her silly jokes and for the moment, I knew I had to enjoy the moment till it lasted.

She pulled out all of her clothes from her wardrobe and shelves, and we tried on all of that, making silly poses in front of the mirror and dancing to the songs that we sang together, giggling and laughing till late at night. We plopped on her bed laughing hard at how crazy we were. I was glad to be in her company. I finally knew what friendship was, and how much it meant and how valuable it was. Maybe not forever but at least for that exact moment, I had forgotten how devastating the situation was. It was a subject of happiness that no matter how dark these peoples' lives were, they had learned to create happiness somehow, out of their dark sides.

To be honest, these people knew what humanity was, more than any other 'normal' person out there.

I stared at the ceiling sighing, trying to hold back my newly formed tears.

"W...what h...happened?" She asked.

"I miss him..." was all that I could whisper.

"M...miss who?"

"Daniel...my boyfriend." I looked to my side, at her smiling a bit, my face turning back to my original state.

"Aah...f...foreigner?" She said smirking.

"Ever fallen in love?" I asked flipping myself on my stomach.

"N...no..." She said. "O...our j...job does n...not permit i...it," she said staring at the space.

"He lives in the United States. I could not talk to him after they kidnapped me, they took away my phone," was all I could say.

"O...oh," was all she said.

I closed my eyes sobbing hard, recollecting his face and the beautiful eyes he had, and all the times we talked over the phone; his voice making my heart flutter, his smiling face etched into my mind making me want to cry even more.

"I regret everything. Going to that bridge, bunking class."

I knew she could not understand anything. But she looked at me, listening to every word I had to say, like a good friend. It was funny though. My classmates would bunk classes every now and then and would still be not caught, but here I was, having ditched my classes just for once, and now kidnapped and in a messed up situation far beyond my zone of belief.

"Do you like this life? Haven't you ever thought of seeking help or running away?"

She shifted uncomfortably and sat up.

"I...i have had...um...th...thoughts about it. B...but the nearby p...police c...comes here t...to the b...brothel f...for service t...to and o...our m...mistress bribes th...them. I...I had m... managed t...to get the n...number o...of the I...IPS officer wh... who h...has the m...merit o.of e...exposing sex r...rackets." She said in a low voice.

"Why don't you call them?" I whispered yelling at her, widening my eyes.

"Th...the m...mistress i...is l...like my m...mother... I...I..." She said with confusion invading her face while I just nodded, understanding her dilemma.

I came to know that there were four other girls who were abducted other than me.

She said that she was confused to call the higher cops because the mistress gave her what she wanted and even sent her for fewer escort services than other girls as she was brought up there and was like a family. That was why other girls were jealous of her, and she had no friends. It was not fair, but I thought it was best to keep quiet.

She could save so many girls from this unjust situation. She could live her dream and inspire many others. I could tell she had secrets that she was unwilling to spill, but then I did not want her to risk herself into doing such a thing. So I kept quiet. There was an eerie silence between the two of us for a while. She was thinking hard about something. I was shocked when I heard her saying suddenly and out of nowhere.

"L...let's do it t...tomorrow m...morning."

I looked at her, my eyes as wide and round as saucers.

I held her hands assuredly saying that we could do it all. We promised to each other that we would be with each other till the end of all this. There is an Indian saying, "Even the walls have ears." but I was unaware of another pair of ears listening to our conversation.

For the first time, I thought that there would be light in our dark lives, but the next morning changed everything...

I woke up to a huge commotion in the next room. Mauni was not beside me. The harsh sun rays of the late morning singeing my skin made me nostalgic of the moments under the banyan tree with my uncle, yet again. I looked at the wall clock and found out that it was nine ten in the morning. I groaned and threw my frame on the bed back to get a little more sleep but sat up in an instant. All the sleepiness vanished from my entire self when I heard a scream from the room next to me. I bet that cracked voice belonged to her.

I ran to the next room and stopped at the doorway, my eyes all wide with horror as I saw her on the floor with tattered clothes and bloody spots and lines all over her face, arms and the exposed parts of her body while the mistress just stood behind the chair, fuming with anger where another Russian sat whipping and beating Mauni. I must have been stupid to have slept through all of this...

"You wanted to go against us?" The mistress screeched.

"Hey! Don't hurt her! Wait! I can..." Before I could say one more word, the man's face contorted with anger and he aimed his loaded revolver at Mauni's head. Everything seemed to be in slow motion. I could see her looking at me with tearful and pleading eyes when I heard a loud bang. I felt my ears hurting causing me to close both of mine with my hands. Everything was a blur. The bullet made an impact throwing her head at the back, causing blood to splatter everywhere. I heard the man chuckling darkly throwing the gun to one end of the room when I ran to her placing her bloody head on my lap, her face barely recognizable from what I had seen the day before.

There was blood on my clothes and on my hands, and on my lap lay an extremely deformed dead body of a girl whom I had managed to be friends with in my entire seventeen years of my life. It did not matter to me to how much blood I was getting on myself. I knew I had failed. I had broken my promise to be with her no matter what. I was screaming and yelling at her to wake up. The truth was too hard to take in. I was slapping her face trying to wake her up even that I knew she was already dead.

I was begging them to call the ambulance but all they did was just look at me mockingly and within minutes, I felt her body temperature going down and her face going pale. I was always scared of dead things especially the fake ones in the movies. But at that moment I realized how horrible it felt to lose a dear one forever, knowing that they are not going to come back ever. I felt that my world was crashing down into dust and ruins. All the hope that I had managed to gather the night before vanished in a matter of seconds and I could not even do anything.

I wanted to hold on to her a little more, but then they snatched her away from me, dragging her body like she was some potato or rice sack while I sat there wailing out loudly. They pulled me again and put me in a cell. I was too upset to think about anything else, too traumatized. I had never seen anything that brutal and cruel before that, and that left me quaking in fear and sorrow. I was to blame. Had I not convinced her to do all such things or emotionally manipulated her, then maybe she would have been still alive, happy and breathing.

I wished I could go back in time and change things, but that was impossible. No one could buy time, not even the wealthiest person on the planet. She was the only spark of light in my life, but I extinguished it myself. And the most pathetic thing was that I could not fight back even if I wanted to.

I felt inferior, weak, scared and blocked out.

It was better for me to keep quiet because I had come to know how these people were; emotionless and insensitive and it was clear that they would not hesitate to kill me. I felt footsteps approaching me, and again, I felt a needle pierce through my skin taking my senses away yet once more.

I woke up later that night. I was wearing a revealing red dress with a high slit, a pair of matching lingerie and stockings. I found that attire ridiculous but I had to keep it on.

I was surprised.

Someone had changed me when I was unconscious.

I knew I was all alone on that journey and I had to do stuff on my own and handle it all by myself. I had gone numb and dead to the world. I was becoming fearless at my ignorance.

They told that I was about to serve an Australian man in his early forties. I was disgusted at how these people supported even pedophilia with open arms just because of some amount of money. It was my first time. Every girl wants her first time to be perfect as per her perspective, and this was not how I wanted it at all. But life had been so harsh on me that I did not care at all.

I went inside the room I was assigned to wait in, and looked around. He was not there yet. I looked at myself in the dressing table's mirror. My lips were stained red, and there was some amount of concealer put on my bruises, maybe in an attempt to hide them. I was forced to chew on a piece of mint flavoured gum, maybe to get rid of my bad breath as it had been more than a day since I had brushed. I started opening the drawers and looking around, exploring certain parts of the room.

The heels had already started killing me even if I had them on for not too long, but I was a slave to them and the situation, so I had to keep them on as long as they liked. It was a good thing that I was getting used to it. The fact that there was a series of heavy knives and loaded pistols in one of the drawers took me by great surprise. There lay a pistol exactly like the one with which they had shot her. I closed the drawer immediately as I heard the door open, revealing a blonde man with sparkly blue eyes. His hair had started turning white, but it was barely noticeable in the dimly lit room. He had a few folds of wrinkles underneath his eyes, and the skin of his hands was a bit loose. He started walking towards me while I looked at him cautiously, directly into his, not letting his eyes waver to anywhere else. I smiled a bit at him, putting my hands behind me as if I was shy.

Yet I had a plan...a very sinister plan...

A plan to kill...

I could have been a great actress. I was profoundly good at acting which I had discovered just then. I was sure that what I was doing was a lot better than those students in school plays because it was working on him.

He chuckled and came closer to me. I felt my back hit the wall when his tall frame leaned down onto me. I felt dizzy from his breath reeking of alcohol. My mind was confused and agitated, just like the ripples in a pond. It was not my choice to decide if I wanted it or not; it was theirs. I was at their mercy even if I owed them nothing.

I had wild thoughts running in my head. I was about to lose my purity to some old man I had never even gotten a chance to talk to or know about, not that I would have done it even if I had gotten a chance. My body, my soul and my entire self, felt revolting against the way he was touching me. I knew I had to decide it right then and there.

My thoughts travelled to the pages of my history book back at eighth grade. The Rajput women used to make a huge pit of fire and jump into it. They did so when the Mughals, who were their sworn enemies, made any unethical move on them for their own satisfaction or pleasure. They would not accept the fact that their enemy or any other man for the matter would touch them the way only their husband had the freedom to. So, before any such thing could happen, they would end themselves in the burning pyre, and that entire course of action was called *Jauhar*.

Now, I was not a sissy girl. I was not willing to accept the fact that I would end myself for the sake of my enemies. Mom used to tell me to be brave and fight back for the right thing and to never surrender to what was wrong. I might not have come under societal influence much, but I was brought up well to be a moral, characterized young woman who believed in proper ethics.

Now people would think I brag a lot about myself but I was and am proud to be who I am and every woman, I say, should feel the same about herself; trying to encourage and empower herself and striving to do something better for her and the people around her.

They said that women were like lotuses while I'd prefer to be a rose; beautiful and bold. A pretty flower indeed, but filled with thorns, pricking those who tried to pluck and destroy her life if not careful.

I knew I would be coiled around my thoughts, confusing myself even more if I started thinking more about that situation and justifying my actions. I did not have much time. It was that I finished either myself or him before something terrible happened.

I was my own person. I had my own choices and decisions. He might have paid a lot of money for getting me, but I knew I was priceless and precious. For the first time, I felt something positive about myself, that I was worth something and that I was valuable to myself first, much before I was to somebody else.

For the first time I felt as if I had the chance to claim myself before anyone took any sort of advantage of me. A chance that I felt, I had to show how I could defend myself in; the sense of freedom amidst the capture.

Time was running out of my hands, just like grains of sand escaping from your fist from the unclosed pores and gaps in between your fingers.

So, instead of thinking what was wrong or right, I decided to do what felt right to me. I brought out my hands from behind and pointed a pistol at his head, straight to the center and gritted my teeth as hard as I could and pushed the trigger twice, just I had seen him kill Mauni, one after the other without any break, blood sprayed all over my face making me flinch a bit as I shrunk my upper torso towards the wall.

I let the gun fall from my hands which were trembling badly.

Everything fell quiet for a second. Even some sort of commotion being created in the place, outside stopped for a brief while.

Mom always relied on things which could be undone and advised me to do the same so that changes could be made whenever wished to, but the fact that I had killed a live human being scared me to the core.

The bold Joan of Arc was replaced by a scared cat in seconds and this was the first time I had killed something huge, alive and breathing. I did something which I had not even thought of doing in my wildest dreams. I knew I was dead for what I did. There was no way I could escape that.

One of the Russian men entered.

He must have heard the gunshot.

He stopped right on his tracks exchanging glances between me and the corpse. His shocked face turned into that of anger and annoyance, and he came walking to me with long strides and held me by the neck, almost choking me. I could not see his eyes as they were well hidden behind those black shades that all the three of them always wore. He threw me against the table, my abdomen making a thudding contact with the pointed edge of the table which made me tear up and heave in pain. He held me by the strap of my dress, holding a gun to my head making me quiver in fear.

The other Russian, the bulky bald man who smelled like a butcher, the same guy who had abducted me from the bridge, placed a hand on his shoulder gently squeezing it. It was as if they were talking through mind link.

The angry man grunted at the Baldie, and he took out his cell and called someone. I looked at the surroundings, scared and embarrassed. There was a group of people by the door, peeking inside trying to catch a glimpse of what had happened, unable to contain in their curiosity.

I could see a man in boxers, his pubic hair jutting out on his inner thighs, from the edges of the underwear he was wearing. He seemed like a customer while squeezed onto him in the crowd was a young girl with smeared makeup all over her face. She had wrapped herself, up in a bed sheet, clutching it tight to her chest, scared that it would slip off to reveal her womanly parts. But at the same time, if they would have worn clothes and then come to see the drama, they would have missed the best part. I could see all those people from the corner of my eyes. Honestly, I wanted to laugh. It was as if an entire circus of Indian b-grade porn stars had come to see the show.

I broke out from the prison of my thoughts when I heard a young male voice answering the call. I could not make out a thing those two were talking about as I knew not a bit of Russian.

I was curious, but I knew it was better to keep shut. I had mentally accepted that they were going to kill me and that was when I heard a dark chuckle from the other end of the line.

I felt a searing pain in my head with the harsh impact of the grip on my skull and everything went black. I swear I saw Mauni smiling sadly at me, standing at one corner and for a moment, I thought she was still alive when I realized I could be hallucinating before everything went black.

The Empire

I woke up after I did not know how long, in a small, dark place. I fluttered open my eyelids to see the two croonies sitting in front of me laughing, talking and munching on something. Maybe they left the third one behind.

I groaned and sat up properly, hissing from the pain in my arm. I looked down to my left hand trying to relocate the source of the pain when I saw an IV needle stuck into my arm, deep into my flesh. My vision trailed from my mid-arm to the pipe, to the tourniquet, and to a hanging net in one corner of the van where there was a transparent bag filled with some unknown transparent liquid which was being pushed into my bloodstream.

I started panicking and looking around like a frightened deer, fearing what was being injected into me. I got a close look at the bag which read 'Sodium Chloride Solution For Iv Injection' along with a long paragraph of its contents, mostly chemical compounds which I had no interest in reading and some date which was very recent and this made me sigh in relief. I looked to my side to see the two guys looking at me having stopped from whatever they were doing.

"What happened?" I asked them shrugging.

They shook their heads, going back to their own hostile severe mode.

"Um...is this needle new or used?" I asked curiously.

"New, not shared," was all I got as an answer.

"I'll kill you if I get any diseases," I told them.

They didn't reply.

I was about to ask them where we were.

"Where are ..." and that is when he threw a bag at me carelessly causing me to yell out loud.

"Hey! Be gentle!"

I groaned making a bothered expression and peeked inside the bag to see some black clothing. I showed the guy sitting next to the driver's seat, my left arm to get the IV out of my arm. He wiped his hands with some med wipes that he pulled out of the van's drawer and held my arm.

His fingers and hands gave out a funny smell combined of both potato chips and some floral or perfume smell from the wipes. He pressed his thumb onto the joint where the needle went inside and pulled it out sharply which made me flinch. He pressed an alcohol-soaked cotton swab on it and asked me to hold onto it for a while till the pain subsided. I waited for a few seconds when he rubbed it on the spot and threw it in a metal bin nearby.

So unhygienic.

I pulled out the content from the bag and unfolded the clothing to find out that there were two pieces of garments, the other one falling to my lap. I raised my arms holding onto it, finding out that one was a big black robe while the other was a *burkha*.

"Are you serious?" I asked them. "Oh come on!" I said looking at them scoffing.

"Change it quick. We don't have much time."

"Tell me! What is going on? Now, which horrible expedition are we going on?"

"Just put it on," he said calmly yet in a dangerous voice.

I knew messing up with them would be bad. I was still in my red dress and without bothering them, I put on the robe over my dress. I was flipping through the drape figuring out how to put that on.

He took the *burkha* from my hand and put it all around my

face and head. My heart sank for a moment. He reminded me of my dad. Even if he had turned out to be not so nice later, he used to wrap a white wet cloth around my face and head when I was a kid before we went out to the outdoors in the scorching hot summer sun to pick up mum from her office on Saturdays when she had a half day.

Being weak and emotional would be futile. There were chances they'd take advantage of me. The world is not as nice as it seems. People are shrewd, cruel and selfish. Sometimes they tend to be so desirous for achieving what they want that they would not hesitate to take advantage of you and your innocence and I could not let that get to me.

He let me out, cuffing me to the door of the van. That was when I realized that we were in some garage or a parking lot, maybe. I heard the van door opening and out came two Muslim guys. I was confused at first. They had dressed up as Muslims. I was an ignorant fool who did not know a fact about what was going on and what irked me the most was their silent treatment. At least they could have given me the minimum information.

"What is happening?" I asked clutching onto one's *kurta*.

All he did was hand me a bag which looked like a satchel. They waited on me as I looked into it. All it had was papers. I was rummaging through the papers unsure of what I was looking for till I felt smaller papers than the ones I had rummaged before. I took it out to see that it was a passport. My passport. A fake one, of course.

I looked at them shocked while he snatched all that away from my hands and started swaggering while I was half hobbling and half running behind them, trying to keep up with them.

"Wait!" I called out to them hissing in pain emanating from my sore and numb legs for having been in the same posture for so long in the van. My body was not permitting me to cope with such sudden changes. But did they wait? No.

Trying to keep up with their long strides, I inadvertently stepped on the robe and fell straight on my face. "Ouch!" I managed to limp and walk up to them and followed them outside to a room which looked like an office. That is when I saw the Russians greeting an old Muslim man. It seemed as if he was around sixty or even older. They were conversing in Arabic from which I could understand a few words but could not fully understand what they were talking about. The old man was looking at me in between their conversations which made me feel uncomfortable. But thanks to my good fortune that the two Russians handed him a bag of cash and we left.

Coming out of the room, I was greeted by the blinding sunlight and the hot afternoon air, plus the black *burkha* I was wearing was making it difficult for me to bear the heat. I turned back and looked up to find a signboard which said,

Ali Khaled Garage Services

near Chhatrapati Shivaji International Airport

Mumbai–400099.

The board was half torn and it was not even straightly fixed. The vibrant blue colour which once might have made the board look beautiful had now faded. The board even had a picture of a bike and an auto at either side of the writing.

I was walking fast to catch up to them but I was mentally screeching, how I had come to Mumbai from Rourkela. We walked for about twenty minutes and walked up on the ramp to the airport. I saw many vehicles entering with baggage, had to be for the other passengers, maybe. I waited in the queue with the Baldie while the other one went somewhere else. There was a long queue of passengers in front of me waiting for their bags to be checked. We had no baggage which panicked me. I saw the other Russian guy talking to some other man at a distance who had around three bags with him. I saw them talking near each other's ears and I saw the Russian slip a thick bundle of notes into his hands and then making his way to us.

He joined behind us on the queue. After checking, we got our bags tagged and he handed me my passport and visa and whatever I needed. I went through the seclusion checking system and came out successful and then I passed the security by showing my visa and passport and they let me through.

I heard the speakers blaring, a woman speaking in a clear voice, "This is the final boarding call for passengers, Timothy Rogers and Freida Richer booked on flight 278A to Tallahassee. Please proceed to gate 4 immediately. The final checks are being completed and the captain will order for the doors of the aircraft to close in approximately five minutes. I repeat. This is the final boarding call for Timothy Rogers and Freida Richer. Thank you."

Tallahassee... that was where Daniel lived. These people were so lucky. I wished I was in their place. I felt a tap on my shoulder. I turned around to see Baldie who grabbed my wrists and made me follow him to the waiting section of gate 3. I was trying my best to manage my robe and not fall down again so as not to get attention. Baldie took me to a seat and asked me to sit down and he sat next to me while the other guy sat on my other side. I sighed at the situation. I was in one of the busiest airports in the world, dressed up in a robe and a *burkha* with two most notorious criminals who killed and did illegal stuff without any remorse or regret and was being smuggled into some other country.

I sighed.

What muck had I gotten myself into? But then I did not want to look or go back again to the life I was living in.

That was when the speakers blared again. A woman spoke, "Good afternoon passengers. This is the pre-boarding announcement for flight 65D to Moscow. We are now inviting those passengers with small children, and any passengers requiring special assistance, to begin boarding at this time. Please have your boarding pass and identification ready. Regular boarding will begin in approximately fifteen minutes time. Thank you."

Baldie looked at me when the woman said 'children'.

"I'm not a kid," I informed him with mocking humor lacing my words making him go back to his original posture once again.

I was looking at the LED television which hung from the ceiling, giving the entire waiting section a posh look along with all the public decor. I mentally hoped we did not look weird. Baldie and the 'other' guy were busy with their phones. Baldie was playing a game, some silly game of a moving snake in a garden which grew longer when you managed to feed it more. I raised an eyebrow at him which he could not see because of my face which was well hidden by the veil.

I saw him fail at a level multiple times. I snatched the phone from him and taught him how to play and completed the level to which he looked at me and the screen alternatively multiple times in awe and surprise. His face looked like that of a kid in a circus. He looked to somewhere over my head to my side and my gaze followed his. The other Russian guy, who was so busy typing furiously on his phone, almost murdering the poor screen, was looking at the Baldie with an angry expression causing him to take the phone away from my hands.

I huffed and crossed my arms and sat on my chair. I was getting bored and restless.

"How much do we have to wait? Ugh!" I groaned. That was when the other guy got up and grabbed my wrist, getting the sling on his shoulder. I saw several passengers which consisted of both white and Indian race getting into the queue under a sign which read gate 3. I even saw a black family standing a few people behind us. I leaned from the queue and looked back at the family of four; all their skins charcoal black and polished. They all looked like a happy family. The father was holding the child on his arms and they were all laughing and chatting. The other kid, a little girl around seven was sipping a drink from the straw from a Starbucks cup which seemed way too big for her. She took huge sips from her drink and handed it to her mother who absent-mindedly took it and sipped on the drink. It was nice watching them share a drink. I guessed I had been watching them for too long as the woman narrowed her eyes and looked at me which made me widen my eyes and I stood straight in my line without looking at them again.

I prayed, mentally wishing she did not see me but I knew for a fact that she did. We made our way into the aircraft through the aerobridge and got onto the plane. Baldie was in charge of displaying any documents they asked for in case. That was when I saw the two properly. Baldie was shorter than the other guy. He must have been around 5'5 whereas the taller guy was around 6'. Baldie and he wore similar kind of black glasses. Baldie's face was full of beard but the taller one only had a bit of stubble and both belonged to Caucasian race. They both reminded me of serious versions of Laurel and Hardy. Well, the Baldie was almost the original version of Hardy except for the beard of course. He reminded me of tough and hard people with brains the size of a pea, with the clueless way he behaved.

The slender guy asked me to sit in the middle seat. I shook my head to show rejection. I could imagine him rolling his eyes behind his glass when he allowed me to pass through him and get the window seat. I saw people still entering the plane. The seats were of economy class or so, I thought. I removed the window shades of the window looking out to the runway when the speakers beeped again and out came the same woman's voice stating to fasten our seatbelts, to secure our luggage and to turn off our cell phones and personal devices, and everybody did so.

The plane took off. The entire time, I felt as if I was weighing five times the weight of all the people causing the tail of the airplane to tilt down.

The speakers beeped again, this time the captain speaking, "Good afternoon passengers. This is your captain speaking. First I'd like to welcome everyone on Rightwing Flight 65D. We are currently cruising at an altitude of 33, 000 feet, at an air speed of 400 miles per hour. The time is 3:45 pm. The weather looks good and with the tailwind on our side we are expecting…" 'blah blah'. Then I saw around three air hostesses coming out from inside the inner cabin and putting on their show as always, directing us to where the safety exits are and all that stuff. It felt somewhat like an annual function in school. The pilot acting like the kid who used to last throughout the program welcoming guests with the speech he had worked so hard upon and sadly to which no one, not even the honorable chief guest paid attention to; trying to update the guests with the upcoming performances. I bet the kid would have taken it all seriously and it was sad how the guests did not pay any attention to all that, but then as every detail, that was necessary too and the program would not seem complete without it. And the air hostesses were like the server girls who served food packets and juice boxes to the participants and other necessary staff, and also like the dancing drill girls who were accurate with each drum beat.

I felt like a secret agent or spy; strong and sturdy yet sly at the same time when I scanned my eyes all over the area. I knew I could see them but they could not, the veil acting as a glass facade. There was an ear-splitting cry of a baby behind me whom the mother was trying hard to shush down. The lucky baby had the air hostesses around her trying to calm her down. 'She must have peed or pooped in her diaper,' I thought. They discovered it after like an eternity which made me sigh. I thought she was more experienced than me but then there, look at what had happened. I saw the woman picking the baby up and making her way to the bathroom, with the baby still wailing, annoying certain passengers while others looked at the baby with awe, admiration, and adoration.

An obese kid was sitting across us, who was sucking on a lollipop as well as chewing on bubblegum vigorously, as if his life depended on it. So that's how kids of this generation welcomed diabetes and rotten teeth with open arms. There was a group of hippie musicians somewhere in front of us who were laughing bizarrely. I bet they were high on drinks or drugs; the way they were laughing, not afraid of showing off their scary yellow teeth which made me barf mentally. There was even a female Christian cleric on the plane. I could see the top of her obnoxiously large religious habit getting in my view. I wondered how she could wear and move around with that massive thing on her head. Maybe, it was easier for God to spot her from heaven that way, as she was considered of a high category and was definitely closer to him. 'Ooof, God needs glasses!'

I slumped in my seat and rested my elbow on the armrest, resting my chin on my palm as I kept gazing out of the window seeing white fluffy clouds all around. I wish I could dive right in and swim within it all feeling like an angel, bursting my wings and flying wherever I wanted to.

That day was quite smooth. They did not act scary at all. I wanted to break free and run off but I could not. I was a murderer. I had blood on my hands; getting caught would be disastrous. But at the same time it was appealing, at least I could have been rescued. I laughed at how I had expected my face to appear on the television under the label "MISSING" in big words, but nothing of the sort happened. The most that could have happened was they would have printed small posters and pasted it all over my town, and the little kids and children would have plucked them all out and made airplanes out of them and flew it to god knows where. At the same time, I did not want to go back to my family, to a series of depressing episodes again so I thought it was best for life to carry me where it wanted to.

A small growl in my stomach interrupted my thoughts. I poked Baldie on his arm as the other one was sleeping or it seemed that way. Baldie gave me a weird look. I went to his ears and whispered, " I'm hungry, you empty brain." He raised an eyebrow at me, probably at my language. He shook the other guy who stirred and woke up shooting an angry look at him. He looked at his watch and pulled out a packet of biscuits. I was in no mood to talk to them or argue with them and create a scene, so I kept quiet and ate them even if they tasted bland, dry and tasteless.

I had a backache from sitting that long. It was weird how the taller guy knew I was hungry. It could be possible though, since he was an expert in medical stuff. I spent two long hours in the plane, looking here and there and sometimes reading the airline issued magazine. I slept after being tired of boredom. I did not watch the television or listen to anything as I was too tired.

After torturous six hours, I heard the pilot saying, " Girls, boys, ladies and gentlemen, we've been cleared to land, please be seated for arrival."

My heart started beating abnormally fast. I was getting anxious. I was in a different country in a different continent and I was unsure about what would happen to me now. The last thing that would happen to me was death, I could think of nothing more.

We got out of the airplane being greeted by the pretty air hostesses who said, "Thank you for traveling with us. Please do travel with us again," showing their straight, perfect pearly teeth. I could even see men drooling over their assets. 'What had gotten into the men of this world?'

I carefully clutched my skirt while walking. My legs were numb from so much sitting, and my head felt a bit dizzy. But I was happy that I had managed to come down, get on the aerodrome to the minibus to the airport.

There was again a long series of procedures at the airport.

Coming out to the exterior, Baldie and the other guy tweaked up their watches according to the big clock in the terminal. There was a long line of a crowd holding placards with their related person's name, their eager eyes scanning the exit way, hoping that they see them soon when they came out. I saw a woman with her kids running towards a man who got on his knees leaving his baggage the way it was and embraced them all at once with his large arms.

Daniel popped into my mind again. We used to talk often about how we would greet each other when we saw each other at the airport; it did not matter if he came to India or if I went to Tallahassee.

He has said that he would have wrapped his arms around my comparatively tiny frame and would have hugged me for a long time. He had said he would have kissed me but I had rejected the idea, stating how much I hated PDA. He had laughed and said that he would kiss me on the cheek or the forehead at least and I had asked him to save that for our alone time together, far away from the crowded world; just us.

It was very funny, how we used to dream so many big things even when we knew that everything was uncertain and that it is all blurry and foggy. But we had promised to try to make it work and prove those people wrong, who used to chant that 'online relationships don't work'.

This was the perfect opportunity to cry. I could do it and no one would see it. There was this mysterious ache in my heart. It was painful in suffering for the consequences of mistakes I never did. I knew that Daniel was slipping off away from my hands and I could not catch him even if I wanted to, the wall of separation was too strong, the evil more potent.

I saw them carrying bags and walking towards me.

I could not hold them back this time. I had to open up my streams before they started overflowing and clogging my entire system. I had a veil in front of my face. I rubbed my eyes from over the veil and patted my face hoping the cloth would soak up all the tears in. There was a line of taxis outside where people were loading and unloading their luggage, going their own ways.

I felt as if I was in an unknown alien world. There were unknown alphabets forming the words I could not understand. People talked in a language unknown to me. It felt as if I had come to visit dad in South India of which's state language I did not know. But then there was no family of mine, here. I was stuck with people I had no idea about. I would have run away but I knew that would have been ruinous for me, so I decided to follow people whom I knew. Baldie had a tight grip on my arm as we went to the parking lot. I felt chilly cold air hit a part of my face making me shiver a bit. There was a man near a mustang there who smiled at the other two.

"Ah! Artyom!" The taller guy among us went to hug him.

Baldie and the other guy took turns in hugging him. We all got into the car and drove off. My spine was hurting really a lot from that posture in which I was sitting in. I was shifting continuously at different angles trying to find a comfortable spot. We had been traveling continuously for about two and a half hours.

The weather seemed as if it was about to rain. It was already evening, the outside barely visible.

We were in the outskirts of the Moscow Federal city. I was still thinking how bold these people were to smuggle people in and out of the country. Searching for me in India was futile and even if they found out where I was, nothing could be done since I was out of the national borders. There were empty plains on either side of the road we were traveling on. It was quite dark outside. I heard the thunder rumbling in the skies above. Raindrops started falling on the exposed skin of my hands which rested on the window pane of the car window. I saw the baby raindrops descending from the sky and bouncing on the window pane and sliding into the unknown alleys of the folds of my robes and vanishing within them. There was an uncomfortable silence in the car. All I could hear was the trees whispering to each other, the sisters of the wind playing with my hair and with the loose pleats of my clothes and my veil.

"Can I take off my veil?" I asked them with a bored voice.

"Oh sweetie, you can," the man with the name Artyom said.

I carelessly pulled it off and held it in my hands.

"You could have at least thanked me for giving you the permission, haven't your parents or teachers taught you manners?" Artyom said looking serious again.

How old did he think I was? Five?

"I don't see why I should thank any of you for being nothing but absolute morons on this planet. And for your kind information, I'm a mannerless bitch to people like you and you can fuck off if you have any problem with it. Kindly do not try to strike a conversation with me, furthermore. Thank you." I retorted.

"Mmm...no wonder why you caught the attention of dear brother," he said smirking.

I was too tired to think of who his brother was or could be. It was already raining hard, the huge raindrops falling and sliding off the glass of car windows which Baldie had closed a few minutes ago. Unable and not trying to comprehend about the situation anymore, I leaned sideways a bit and rested my head on the window of the car. The muffled sound of the pitter patter of the water globules lulled me to sleep.

I woke up with my head hitting on the glass of the car when it received a bump.

"Ow," I said rubbing my head with my palm.

Artyom chuckled.

"It's not funny! Don't you know how to drive a car?" I said.

"Not my fault if the road has bumps in it," he said.

"Whatever," I said slumping back in my place.

The rain had stopped. I slid down the windows of the car.

The air was fresh and the smell of the rain invaded my nostrils.

We passed through a few villages and small towns on our way to a place called Pegrema.

We had to pass through dirty alleyways and filthy streets to make way to our destination. I could see small shops with rusty doors and dirt stained walls so dark that one could mistake those for coal stains. The fresh air was replaced with a putrid and dirty smell. There were dustbins at some corners which were carelessly thrown around, garbage spilling out from them. Scrawny stray dogs were sniffing at the garbage in hope of finding something to feed on while some chasing the poor black cat which belonged to nobody probably. The buildings had two to three storeys at most with no space between them. It was almost as if two buildings shared a common wall. I could see dull and almost dead faces of the inhabitants looking down at the streets. There was no colour, just depressing shades of darkness and dullness. There was no happiness. I could smell death and morose in the atmosphere. It looked like a place where goons of the eighteenth or nineteenth century would have resided. I even saw two ghastly men holding a knife to a man's neck who was helplessly begging them by joining his hands while one of them was robbing him. Even if we passed quickly enough, there was no way I could not see all that was happening here. My eyes met with that of a lady's, wearing black lipstick who seemed as if she was ready to pounce upon me.

The rainwater had washed down the concrete roads making the atmosphere look darker and the chilly atmosphere was bound to send chills through the spine of any spectator who passed through. It was as if I was witnessing a trailer of some extreme criminal or gangster movie.

It almost felt like the old dirty hidden streets of London in Oliver Twist.

Artyom took a sharp turn which made me feel as if the car door would open and I would fall down to the streets and devoured by these hungry wolves whom I witnessed a while ago. I sighed in relief to notice that the child lock was on and that I was safe. I welcomed the natural smell of fresh trees and grass with much happiness. The entire place looked like that of the countryside; Lush, green and beautiful but holding deep secrets within. Secrets I was going to be a part of.

It was pretty late at night and I was tired of traveling so much. The only source of light was the light from the headlights.

"How long do we have to travel?" I whined.

"Not long, sweetheart. We are almost home," he said smiling.

Home, my ass.

I thought about my home back in India. It was a home just for name's sake. Let's say I was a homeless tramp who was yet to find a home where she felt she belonged and actually could get that warm welcoming feeling that military people described like when they returned "home" to their family and relatives.

I looked at the windscreen when Artyom slowed down the vehicle. There was a muddy path to our left with green fields surrounding it. My poor vision could make out the outlines of mountains and tall trees, or maybe I was seeing things in the dark. We came to a halt at a big iron gate which looked very old. Artyom whistled. He craned his neck out of the window.

"EGOR!" He yelled.

I could not understand at first what it meant. I thought it meant "open" but later I found out that it was the name of the guard.

"Welcome to 'The Empire'." He said, his lips curling up into a mysterious smile which did not fail to make my heart skip a beat.

Hell and the Devil

We pulled up at the huge mansion which belonged to their so-called 'brother' or 'master' for whom they loved to work as slaves. Everyone got out of the car except for Artyom who drove to our left. I did not know anything about the place or what to expect so I thought it was best to follow what the others were doing. I waited with them under what seemed like a pomegranate tree. We saw Artyom walking to us and leading us to inside the mansion.

Baldie had a strong grip on my arms. I rolled my eyes at how stupid he was. He should have known by then that it was not possible for me to escape from a place I knew nothing about especially at that time of the night. Maybe, he did it to make things extra sure and safe.

We passed through a couple of rooms, most of which were locked. Every single object, every single thing gave out an expensive vibe. The man had to be rich, either a hardworking man or some useless fellow showing off his ancestral property in which his contribution would have been almost...nil.

I was oddly calm for my original self. I tended to panic for the simplest things. But this time I was calm. It almost felt like I was about to go up to the stage for a debate or an elocution contest.

As a child, I would find it really weird when the teachers would send me for such competitions just because I could speak in two accents, one was the normal Indian one which I used to find boring and cliché and the other one was half American and half British which I had worked really hard on to make it perfect and it was something which my teachers and friends found really cool.

I had a poor memory though. I would sit in my room for hours practicing the five-minute speech I would have prepared, with so much difficulty, going through thousands of books and internet articles till I felt I was ready and capable of doing anything in the world. I would then arrive at the spot twenty minutes before the appointed time (blame that on my mother's over obsession for being punctual) and walk around the compound of the contest venue feeling smart and confident.

Then some or the other student would show up from some high-class school in some expensive car in a crisp shirt and with a studious expression with several papers in his hands, walking but with his gaze still fixed on the papers and I would feel as if I had not prepared well. So I would get back to some place where I could sit comfortably, most of the times the comfortable place being the cemented platform around the trees in schools, from which I would just roughly blow away the dust and sit down again for revising.

It would be so boring since I would have learned everything by then. The bubbles of my confidence would keep on popping until there was none left when I would see such fluent and excellent performances.

I would get the first blow of nervousness when the host would loudly call out my name followed by thundering claps echoing all around the big hall and for the moment, my once confident self would be then replaced by one of anxiety, and fear. I would mumble and stutter whatever would come into my mind, making an utter fool out of myself. I would see some kids laughing and snickering while the judges in the panel would be making a disgusted face at me. I would try to stutter out a thank you and leave complaining about how unfair life was and all of my pathetic excuses would never fail to expand themselves into the little universe inside my mind.

I knew I would freak out, so I was better prepared or maybe I would not. There was not an audience here, besides this was some serious situation going on where I had no second chances.

Artyom opened a door which had the word 'Sinteraction' carved out in fancy cursive. He switched on the lights and it looked like any other bedroom. It was well lighted with modern fan and air conditioning system. Thin translucent curtains framed the windows. The room was too good to house a hostage. I felt as if someone was watching me from behind causing my head to turn around. I narrowed my eyes to adjust my sight but thanks to my horrible eyesight I could see nothing.

I turned back to the three guys. I was shocked when I saw Artyom lift up the upper half of the bed in the room, which was actually hollow. I could make out a rectangular outline. There was a metal lever at the right wall of the wooden hollow. He held the handle of the lever and pulled it hard. It did not budge at first. He felt the wooden panel and lifted a lid which was well camouflaged with the setup. It was a biometric device. Maybe it was a sensor equipped device. I saw a red light beeping and Artyom pressed his finger on the panel. There was a creak and the outline now descended down to a flight of stairs.

Baldie and the other guy stepped into the box carefully and walked down the stairs to the dark interior. I looked down there and back to Artyom, hesitant to go inside it.

"It's all fine sweetie," he said. "Are you scared of the dark?"

I threw him a look and got to the stairs. The smell of rusty metals hit my nose. I covered my nose and looked around while getting down. Rest of the stair steps were made up of metal, except for the initial ones which were made of wood. It looked like some car workshop. Chains were hanging from the ceiling, whips decorated the walls, and there were belts of all sizes. The ground was hard; it felt as if it was made up of concrete.

I could see motorcycle and car tyres lined up at one side of a wall. There were a lot of tables. The weird thing about those tables was that they were fixed to the ground. It was like an extremely modified form of a basement. It was a settlement ideal for prisoners.

We were underground. Everything was dim and dull. The lighting was depressing. The room seemed to have sucked the life out of me in such a short matter of time. Imagine what it would do if I stayed here for weeks or months or worse, for years.

"Everything good?" Artyom yelled from the top.

"Da!" Baldie yelled from below, where we were.

Those were the first words I heard from Baldie.

"Let me show you around," the other guy said to me.

The fact that they were opening up to me was rather relieving and less scary.

There were several rooms except for the room in which people arrived.

A kitchen, a shower with a toilet attached, the meeting place was what they called a room with a big round table having chairs at both sides, and four bedrooms. It looked like a metal version of a large family dining table meant for lavish dinner purposes.

The entire area smelled of bleach and chlorine. The walls were made of metal. The entire place was eerie looking and oddly cold. It had a vibe of the morgue house but without the dead bodies. The entire place was devoid of windows.

"How the hell will I breathe when there are no windows?" I asked them shocked and worried.

"I'm not at liberty to answer to your questions," the other guy yelled from the kitchen. I could hear the clanking of glasses which made me think that he was probably fixing himself a drink.

"I'm sleepy," I said yawning.

Baldie motioned me to follow him. We were heading towards the bathroom which got me cracking into madness.

"I said I wanna go to sleep, not to pee"

But would he listen? No.

I dragged my feet behind him, following him to the bathroom. Ever heard of people say "Everything is possible." ? Well, this was how they were proving it to me. You can really expect anything to happen in a house which has a secret trapdoor with biometric access.

He opened the bathroom door with a thud and went inside while I stood at the door like a nice polite young lady. Out of curiosity, I held onto the wall and peeked in the bathroom where another shock awaited me. I saw Baldie counting the tiles and truth to be told, he looked like a kid in the fifth grade who usually scratches his head and stare into blank space, pondering a lot over questions like,

2+2=__

"You're not being serious, are you?" I asked him throwing an unbelievable look.

"For God's sake someone wants to sleep and you are here counting the number of tiles in the bathroom?" I could not help but raise my voice a little though every moment made me tremble like a scared cat.

I knew that even a small mistake could contribute to my murder and no one would know. I was well concealed in some country no one in my family could think of, in their wildest dreams, or even me for the matter.

But I was frustrated. I had a pounding headache and I was starving.

I saw him getting close to a specific spot in the bathroom and push a tile which looked like any other tile embedded on the bathroom wall. My eyes popped out of my sockets when I saw that one block go in and come back to its original place. Then a huge block of tiles got in and slid inside to a side revealing a space which looked like a doorway. Baldie looked back at me to find a transfixed and a frozen me with eyes wide and a gaping mouth.

"Inside," he said with an innocent voice.

I thought that his voice would be rougher as per his appearance. He looked like a buff elderly man with a voice that of a small child.

I wanted to laugh but my mind was overpowered with what had just happened.

Who were these people?

Why such sophisticated technology in such a traditional dwelling?

Who was the mastermind?

What did they want?

As weird as it sounds, I was tired but not tired at the same time. Well, we can put it up this way, my body was tired but my mind was not. I wanted to explore more but I guess I was not at liberty to do that.

"You better come in or you sleep on the bathroom floor," he said.

I frowned and stomped my way into the doorway.

"Suka..." He muttered.

I stopped there and looked at him.

"Sorry, what?"

"Just go inside before I drug you again."

I was barely inside when he pushed me in causing me to fall down and into a room. Before I could get up and look back, I heard a loud thud. I looked back and saw that the doors were closed. My heart was hammering in my chest. I had never been alone all along in this journey. The fact that I was in a room all alone was alone freaking me out. All I could see was that I was surrounded by thick walls around me.

I could not help but cry. I was habituated of living at home all alone but I was scared this time. Maybe because I did not feel protected. I could not help but break down. The nostalgia was too much. The negative side of my life had won each time, and here I lay, helpless and broken. I was screwed in my mind.

After a while of emotional bumps and breakdowns, I decided to look around the room and see if I could find something new and interesting as I had still some energy left in me to keep me going. The room I was in had no ventilation or windows. We were under the soil and it was obvious not to have any such mechanism. I looked up to find a few square openings which were well meshed with welded rods. There was a weird whirring noise coming from up there but it was impossible for me to find out as the ceiling was too high for me to reach up to.

The room I was in was actually better than the ones which I

had encountered a while earlier. The walls were painted with a pale yellow colour. The smell of the paint was still lingering in the air. The room seemed to have been closed for too long just after being constructed. I could feel grains of sand and dust particles under the thin soles of my shoes when I rubbed my footwear clad feet on the ground.

I missed my old shoes, the one I always wore. Mom would always offer me to buy a new pair but then I'd always stick to it.

The bed in the room smelled musty and old. There was a cupboard in my room which I was too tired to explore then, so I plopped into the bed and fell into a deep siesta, not reacting to the smell it bore because I was too tired to do anything else.

I woke up after I do not how much time. I wished I could I see the time or check it but I did not have a watch nor could I find a clock anywhere. I stretched myself a bit to get rid of laziness and removed the crust from the corner of my eyes. I knew my breath smelled bad and I was wondering what could be next.

I banged on the camouflaged area where the doorway was earlier but got no response. I had nothing to do either when the idea of the cupboard struck my mind. I made my way to the cupboard and was about to open it when I heard the same sliding noise.

My instincts told me that opening the cupboard was not the right thing to do, that it was forbidden and wrong to explore it. In order to avoid trouble, I scurried to the bed and acted like I had just woken up and were stifling a yawn. I saw Baldie opening the door. He strode towards me with long steps making me scared for a moment. He grabbed my hands and dragged me out of the room like a kid dragging a rag doll.

"Hey! Ease down!"

But he did not pay any heed to me as usual.

We surpassed the bathroom and were once again in the common room. I was welcomed by numerous pairs of curious eyes staring at me. The room fell silent for a moment. I mentally counted and found out that there were six other teenagers excluding me of somewhere around my age and a lot of other people who were dressed exactly as Baldie and the other guy who had escorted me. There were even three women among all those people and what creeped me out was that they all had their eyes covered with the shades of the same kind of glasses.

"What?" I looked at them.

All the hostages including me were given a small backpack. I even saw the chairs around the large table had our names carved on them. Even the plain black backpacks that we were given had our names sewed on them. My eyes met with a pair of green eyes of a handsome guy. He smiled gently at me. I thought of Daniel at the moment. I smiled a bit at him when a lady slapped his head yelling, "Focus, Romeo!" causing the rest of the elderly people to chuckle.

"Now find your seats and sit down!" The same lady said in a loud booming voice.

Her voice was bold enough to even to scare a lion away.

The room was filled with the sound of feet shuffling around as other hostages started searching for their seats frantically. I looked around a series of names and finally found mine.

I had barely gotten into my seat when the room fell silent all of a sudden. I saw several people looking at the folding staircase which lay behind the table and which then was beside the seat. I looked at the stairs to find a slender man standing, only the area of from his knees and shoes visible. His shoes were shining from the light in contrast to the darkness his upper body was in.

A man descended down the staircase in formal clothing and a coat.

Our eyes met for a while and an unknown feeling washed over me. A feeling of strange comfort and warmth. I felt ridiculous of my own thoughts.

"Stop thinking or feeling that, you despo," I scolded myself.

He kept staring at me for a few seconds before I pulled away my gaze looking elsewhere.

"Now now, what do we have here?" He said grinning devilishly showing off his teeth which looked pretty weird. Within moments, the warmth was gone which felt strange. It was almost as if I wanted it to come back.

He had braces on his uneven shark-like teeth. I did not see the point of him wearing braces, not that his teeth were protruding out of his mouth, they were just not leveled. I wondered how he managed to keep them all in his mouth even though I admit they were not that long, they were pretty short but I was curious if it hurt his lower gums to possess such teeth.

He wore a crisp white shirt and black pants. The way he was addressing and walking down, looking as vain as a peacock assured me that he was the mastermind of the whole game.

I grit my teeth out of anger. He was responsible for me being here, the reason I could not talk to Daniel anymore, the reason I was in this not so normal situation anymore.

Not that I wanted to be in a normal situation anyway...

I was looking down blankly at the table when I heard people gasp. At the far end of the table stood a black guy and a white girl who had a shaved head.

They seemed not to have been able to find their seats. She looked weak though. She had black squared glasses on and looked clueless as to where to go.

Was she blind?...

I heard something click and I looked at the man who just had come down, aiming a gun at either of them. Two people in the uniform held them tight so that they won't run away. The black guy started crying out loud.

It seemed he had been through enough and it was difficult for him to carry on any longer.

"Don't!" I yelled looking at him when he was just about to pull the trigger.

"Don't kill them, please! I'll pay for their consequences. Just please don't hurt them," I said pleading to the man.

He chuckled and came near me. I could smell his strong cologne and the smell of aftershave was devouring my senses.

He held my hair tight and yanked it back so that I could face his tall self. I was a helpless rabbit in the clutches of a hunter.

He trailed the gun along my jaw smiling darkly.

"Look who's here. Quite a savior now, aren't you? You wanna pay for the consequences of their doings? Eh?"

"Yes, I do"

"What a brave, brave girl. Well, suit yourself," he said tilting his head to another side looking serious trailing the cold gun on my lips, parting them slowly.

I squeezed my eyes shut. I bet he was about to shoot my face. Everyone was looking at me with shock and horror, at least the ones I could see then.

I was craving for the unspoken and unexpressed warmth again, at least once before I died. I was looking directly into his eyes searching for that hidden source of comfort before closing them and preparing for what was about to come.

And now here I was, going to die for two helpless people. I was happy I was doing such a brave deed but at the same time, I was trembling.

At least two people would remember me for saving their lives...

Would it hurt bad?

Will I feel anything?

Will I go to heaven or hell?

That's when I heard a gunshot. I swear my ears rang for a while. I felt nothing. No pain or hurt.

My eyes teared up as a wave of memory hit me hard, the time when Mauni was shot.

I felt nothing.

I opened my eyes slowly. My hair was still in his grip; luckily it did not hurt much now. I thought I was in heaven but I was dead wrong. I strained to look at my side to see the bald-headed girl not standing there anymore whereas a few people were leaning down. I wanted to see more but the tall guy made me look at him.

I stared angrily at him.

"I think I told you I wanted to pay for them?"

He leaned closer to my ear and said in a low voice, "I don't punish people for mistakes they never did."

He pushed me to the chair and walked off upstairs, probably for getting out.

"I'll be back for the introduction session. Get rid of the body of the dead girl." That's all he said.

There were whispers and chattering about what had just happened. For some reason, I felt that I was being given extra attention and I did not know why.

The lady came to the table and rapped it hard causing everyone to shut up.

"You will do exactly what you are said to do or else you'll be..... shot," she said in a loud clear voice emphasizing on the last word.

Their boss surprisingly had a clear American accent. I bet he was some rich spoiled goon from some other country, most probably from the United States who had these people employed from their native lands.

We were standing in a line after the orders and were given time to talk to others. The girls were looking at me and talking about something by whispering into each other's ears and I was cent percent sure it was related to what had happened a while before. I felt miserable that I could not save the girl. I was standing randomly when I saw the green-eyed gorgeous guy approaching me.

"Hello," he smiled.

"Um...hi," I said rather shyly.

"I'm Edvin,"

"I'm Asha,"

"How old are you?"

"I'm 17 and what about you?"

"Oh, um...I'm 19."

"Cool,"

"Do you know why we are here?"

"I wonder about it too. Honestly, I thought I was kidnapped or something but...this is something weird, a facility or a mass kidnapping, maybe?"

"Yeah...and that was a...um... a brave face that you showed there... You did not seem fazed by it.....by the way, do you know anything else about this place?"

I was getting annoyed by the way his approach was. It was as if he was randomly trying to dig information out of me.

He should have understood that I came along around the same time as him. How would I know more than him that he was asking me?

"I appreciate what you think about me but can I be please left alone?"

I walked away from him and stood near the bathroom door.

I was getting impatient. There was this one guy inside who was taking too long while the others were banging and yelling.

He came out after what seemed like a hundred years, earning angry glares from other guys.

A girl, a brunette to be exact, strutted up to me. Attitude was radiating out of her like radiation from some nuclear reactor. She flipped her hair and stood before me.

"Um...can you just move away, please? I'm going in first."

Placing a hand on my hip I said, "And why would I let you go in first when I have been standing here for the last forty minutes in the line? You better go stand behind me before someone else comes, if you wanna be quick, I'm not letting you get in front of me."

"Try me, bitch," she said forcing herself into the spot in front of me only to get thrown out by me.

She gave me an annoyed look and I could not hold back my temper. I held her by her hair and banged her head across the wall and the weakling fainted. There were gasps all around me while the lady with the loud voice ran into the area and looked sharply at me.

"Stand right there," she said going behind the wall maybe to the kitchen while I stood there looking at the faces of the other kids who kept on staring at me.

"Why y'all looking at me like that?" I yelled.

She came back and said, "Well, miss bossy, stop doing what you're not authorized to do and follow me like a nice, well behaved lady before something really bad happens to you."

Wow, that must have been the nicest thing she must have ever said.

I followed her first to the kitchen and then back to the room which had the long table where the girl had died. They had wiped off the area clean. I was sure they had a degree in cleaning.

She started ascending the stairs, the stairs through which I had got in.

I stopped following her and she looked down to me.

"Where are you taking me?"

"To where you are ordered to be right now."

"And what place would that be?"

"You are not supposed to know that just yet."

"Why should I trust you?"

"Do I care? You are forced to follow them and it is not your place to question us," she said pointing her gun at me. "Now better follow me before something terrible happens."

There goes the signature line.

"Fine," I said sighing and a bit irritated at the same time.

I was taken aback when she turned to her right where we were supposed to turn left for opening the trapdoor. She slid aside the curtains and pressed her fingers on a box like object which was barely visible due to the lack of lighting. I saw green neon light in the form of fingerprints and a door slid across when we passed through it. We emerged to what looked like a pantry. It was freezing cold to where we emerged. There were shelves of food and fresh produce at our sides.

"Where are we?" I asked.

She said nothing and kept on walking and we stopped in front of a metallic door. She pushed it with a little force and it opened. We emerged again into a kitchen where we saw an old woman and a skinny girl working. They stopped their work and looked down when she led me into it. They looked at me and I smiled at them. They looked like the most peaceful creatures I had encountered till then.

The old woman kept looking down but the girl looked at me and smiled a little waving her hand a little. The lady with me stopped walking and looked back at her which caused her to look down immediately to her chopping board.

There were neatly arranged utensils on the shelves and the girl seemed to be cutting some chocolate bar into small pieces while the woman had flour all over her apron, who seemed to be rolling out some pastry dough. The entire place smelled of food, like some kind of broth or soup being cooked. She started walking again and I followed her. I had tears welled up in my eyes.

The girl in the kitchen had reminded me of Mauni. We climbed up a fleet of stairs and walked across a hallway. There were rooms on either side, which were locked. It looked like a haunted place, ancient and dusty. We stopped at the last door of the hallway. The wood was black, may be made of ebony which made it stand out from the other doors. There was a beautiful rose carved on the door.

The lady with me knocked softly on the door.

A familiar voice said, “Let her in.”

The lady looked at me with disgust and irritation. She reminded me of the jealous girls in school when I won a literary award or when something really good happened to me, which kind of left me confusing.

I opened the door and got in.

The boss, or whatever he was called, was standing facing the window. I did not realize it was already dark by then. It was not totally blue, but more like the ultramarine blue color that used to happen to be present in my set of fifty oil pastels far long ago when I used to go to art classes as a kid. My favorite hour, the hour between the night and the dusk.

Sunset was okayish for me. The bright hues of fuchsia, orange and red painting the sky with their brilliant beautiful hues. But those colours never were much to my liking as they were too bright and sometimes, I felt hot and sweaty at that hour. But this was just perfect. All cool and not really dark. It kind of complimented my personality, maybe?

There was a leafless tree out there and a few birds were flying in the sky, perhaps going to their nests for gaining back their graceful vigor for the next morning; so that they could fill the atmosphere and the world with their little delightful chirpings and noises again, alerting the world that it was morning again, indirectly embracing us with their sweet melodious natural voices.

"So...it's you," he said still looking out of the window.

I could not see my surroundings well. There was an electronic chandelier on the ceiling but the lights were off, just a bit coming into the room from outside.

"Sorry sir...?" I tried saying with some respect even if I had none in my heart.

"Isn't it beautiful?"

"Yes, it is sir."

"Hmm..." He said inhaling deep and exhaling and I could hear that very clearly.

I kept looking down, a bit nervous in the presence of this heartless man who bore such monstrosity in himself.

"You're the one who woke me up that night from my sleep."

"Sorry sir, but I don't understand what you're talking about."

"What an interesting girl.....was not it you who murdered the Australian man?"

Everything that I had managed to bury so deep in my heart starting spilling out, the blood, the screams, the unfair treatment, the brutality.....everything.

"Yes sir, that was me." I spoke confidently, suppressing it all in me.

I knew that fear fed the negative energy. I was not going to exhibit that.

"Doesn't blood faze you anymore, my dear?"

I tightened my lips in disgust hearing that coming out from him.

"Actually it does but I'm unsure of it now."

I was actually thinking of how I might have awoken this creep when I remembered the phone call of that night.

Oh, so it was him whom the two morons had called after I had killed the pedo.

"Mhm.....so we have a bold chick here, eh? How about something a bit scarier? To lessen down all that remaining fear?" He smiled evilly.

The atmosphere in the room was enough to give me chills and now, what this guy wanted from me?

He turned around and looked at me, and started coming closer.

I could make out his silhouette in the dark, the dim yellow light illuminating his hidden face as it came into my view.

He looked rather weird. His face appeared somewhat wrinkly and he pulled out his hair which shocked me.

It had been a wig all this while?

It turned out that he had been a bald man all this while.

He was drawing closer to me, grabbing a tiny remote kind of thing in his hand while backing down till he was so close to me that our bodies were almost touching and I could not really run because there was a thick wall behind me.

I closed my eyes in fear and nervousness despite the fact that he smelled good. Thousands of horrible possibilities started running through my mind forcing me to squeeze my eyes shut and look sideways, squirming beneath him.

He pressed the button with a beep and I could feel that the lights were on. I had never been close to a man before and there were hoards of things going on in my mind by then that I was not able to think straight.

"Open your eyes!' He yelled. " Or else!" I could feel something cold on my temples which made me open my eyes in an instant.

I wanted to scream to what I saw in front of me.

The man in front of me had a natural human body but his

face.....it looked horrifying.

His eyes were puffy and red. It seemed as if he had been crying. His red ears and inflated face confirmed my suspicion. The skin on his face was spiky and green in certain places and his lashes were white and abnormally long as if he was wearing fake lashes.

I extended out my trembling hands and tried to pluck out his eyelashes to confirm my hypothesis.

"You dare do that girl?" He said covering his eyes and that's when I saw his hands of the same texture and they did not have nails. It was empty there, just a light depression of where they would have been.

He put both of his hands beside my head so that I could not escape.

What was wrong with this guy?

Why is he so confusing?

Even though my face was white as if I had seen a ghost, I was on my guard because of his unpredictable behavior.

I was legit mentally prepared to be killed.

He looked beautiful as that, like some piece of art. Unusual and different, representing uniqueness...

I mentally shook my head scolding to myself about what I was thinking. My fingers were itching to touch his grainy and spiky skin.

"C...can I touch it?" I asked for permission, my fingers already half the way to touch his skin.

He said nothing, just kept staring into my eyes. As much petrified I was, I was willing to explore what was held in his orbs. He was heterochromic. One was a green eye while the other was yellow, or golden should I say, just like a wild wolf's eyes.

His green orbed eye was beautiful as if thousands of evergreen forests had cluttered themselves into that one circle. It sparkled like an emerald.

His pupils were dilated.

His other eye was beautiful too, just like sparkling amber resting in the deepest depths of the ocean. His eyes seemed like they had an unknown spark in them at that moment. I could feel and as if I could almost see the emotions flowing out his eyes for which I had a feeling, it was quite rare.

There was hurt, sorrow, anger, desire, hunger and so much more. I placed my hands on his cheek cherishing the rough and spiky feeling. It felt as if I was rubbing my palms across an acupressure pad.

I was surprised to see him closing his eyes and pressing his face closer to my palms. I could feel it was a bit sticky, maybe from the adhesive used for his prosthetic makeup; the same kind of glue my mom's bindi had.

As unexpected it was, he opened his eyes and lowered his lashes to my lips and decided to lean closer making me look sideways. As weird as it was, it felt somehow right. The truth was easier to accept when I thought about it. The thought of Daniel came faintly flashing in my mind. There was no doubt he would have moved on. Who would stay in an online relationship without response and hope? The painful yet true fact seemed easier to accept. I could feel the warmth radiating off his body and enveloping me within its invisible arms. My mind was in a jumble of thoughts but the feeling that it was alright, kept me going.

My eyes opened in shock when he grasped his fingers tightly around my neck.

"Scream!" He yelled at me.

"Scream, scream, scream! Aren't you scared? Scream!" He bellowed.

"I'm not scared of you?" I said it more like a question but for his satisfaction, I screamed loudly for whole fifteen or twenty seconds.

"That's unnatural! You don't mean it!" He screamed at my face shaking me violently. Before I could think more, I was flung to the wall on the other side of the room.

The color of the room was maroon and there were the pictures of Russian revolutionaries hung on the top of the wall. There were black decorated wall curtains which seemed to be of velvet. I felt something trickling down my forehead. I touched it and I saw blood on my fingers. I felt too weak; the walls were closing down on me. But before everything went black, I felt the same grainy hands cup my face. And that was when I knew, this was the hell and that I was in the clutches of the devil.

Guests at the Party

I woke up in the lower bunk bed in one of the rooms in the basement. The sheets felt cold against my skin. The smell of metal got to me, making me groan a bit. I had a splitting headache. I touched my forehead realizing that I had a bandage wrapped around it. I managed to sit up and look down at myself. I smelled good and I was dressed in a pair of loose capris and a black t-shirt. I wondered who changed me.

Unable to strain my head anymore, I got down from the bed and walked out of the room. The long round table was occupied. Every chair was occupied except for three chairs which were mine and the nameless one's, next to mine which seemed to be the extreme one at one end of the table. The other chair named "Emma" was empty too, the seat of the girl who was shot on the first day by that monster.

I walked slowly and made my way to my seat. The lady who had escorted me earlier looked at her watch on her wrist. I was curious, what the time was and I knew it would be useless asking her so I decided to keep quiet.

My mind traveled all the way to what had happened some time ago.

What was going on?

What did it all mean?

Was that some disease or something?

Was it contagious?

Did I get it too since I was near him?

For every new possibility that arose in my mind, it freaked me out more.

The chattering fell to a hush which made me snap out of my thoughts. I saw him coming down the stairs again.

"Young ladies and gentlemen, welcome to another living nightmare. Aren't y'all lucky enough to have been given the opportunity to be my test subjects?" He smiled maliciously.

Oh dear, here we go.

Wait, What?

"So, you're some scientist or something?" Someone asked, far away from me. I craned my neck to see who it was but I guess I still could not figure it out.

The freak aimed his gun at the kid and shot him, making our ears ring a little.

It was a small boy.

Wait, when did he get here? He wasn't there when we were sitting here last.

He must have been around seven.

It wanted to read the name but my vision was not clear since I didn't have my glasses on.

Everyone was trembling on the table while the girl in front of me had tears rolling down her cheeks.

Yi Ling. Poor kid.

"No questions before you're given the permission to," he said. His voice could be compared to that of a panther: graceful, slow, quiet but never failing to get to their victim.

And by the way, who kills someone for such a puny thing?

Then suddenly something struck my mind.

Maybe that was not a disease at all. What if there was an accident during his experiments?

That must have driven him insane.

I heard the chair near me shift. I saw the devil sitting to my left.

Oh good lord, why?

Everyone was looking at him while I was staring down at my hands on the table.

"Eyes towards me when I talk," I heard him say close to me. I looked up to find everyone looking at me. I looked at him curiously. I was shocked to see his face. His prosthetic makeup made his face look a lot more realistic.

I could still imagine his spiky face beneath all those layers of makeup. Or maybe, I could because I knew what was beneath all that.

Those beautiful eyes hidden beneath those brown lenses.

It was not my fault I found weird things pretty.

I looked at him forcefully. But instead of looking at everyone else, he kept on looking into my eyes and saying everything.

"There are ground rules, if not followed strictly; you know what your punishment is. You will be doing exactly what the officers say."

Officers, my ass. What a decent way to call bad people in uniforms.

"You should not try to escape. Else we will blow up your families and you don't want that now, do you?"

"And you are here for conduction of several experiments."

"The person who survives them all will be given a life to live as per his or her wish."

It was all confusing. Test subjects from other countries. Now this man had brains. Of course, you could smuggle people and do whatever you want with them and the country could not do anything since you were out of the borders for the law to be followed.

No wonder this wicked headed man was like this. I bet if he would have used his IQ and intelligence in good projects, the world would have been a lot more benefitted by them.

I was curious about what had caused him to be like this? What was the mystery behind it all? And why did I feel as if he was favoring me? The way I was being reckless, I would have been finished a long time ago. I did not care about life anymore.

But life was life. People may place their opinions but events in life are inevitable. No matter how much you shouted or how much you whined or complained about it, things will happen the way it happens and one cannot really change it.

I was feeling uncomfortable under his continuous burning gaze. I wanted to slap the shit out of him but I could not because after whatever I thought, I still did not want to die, at least not knowingly.

I sighed in relief when he looked away from me to others.

"How about we come to know about you all?" He cracked an evil grin.

Oh jeez, keep that attitude to yourself.

He snapped his fingers and the lady who had not been so nice to me for the last few days handed him a thick file and a black spectacle case.

"Thank you, Anechka," he said.

I could not help but snicker. I found the name quite funny. Maybe, that was because I did not come across it often and was not used to hear such kind of names.

I realized that I had just laughed.

Oh, shoot.

He looked at me with a grave expression on his face, both his eyebrows lifted up.

I knew I was dead. My death was drawing near.

I was shocked at what he said next,

"I found the name quite funny at first too."

There were whispers all over the room. The people in the room looked dumbfounded at what just happened. I was shocked, myself. I bet any other person who would have done it would have gotten shot. As much relieved I was, it felt wrong as if something unfair was going on. I felt a part of an unjust transaction. The girl whom I had knocked off near the bathroom looked happy at first but now, her face looked as if a wave of disappointment had washed over her. I just prayed that my guts were in control.

"Now getting back to where we were. How about we start with the deceased?"

I did not trust this guy. He could be quiet at first but a killing machine the very next moment. And I would not be able to do anything but sit there while he instantaneously killed me, and nothing could ease down the fear.

He opened the spectacle case and put on his spectacles. Now, he looked like a really innocent salesman or a nerdy banker, maybe.

He opened the book and flipped a few pages till he was almost somewhere in the central part of the thick file. It had so many printed pages, the initial pages looking yellowish and torn a bit at the edges but, they were well maintained. There were pictures too. I wanted to see them but I had to contain my curiosity in.

There goes the information of the guests and the hosts of the party.

Emma Williams: A thirteen-year-old from Leicester, United Kingdom. She was blind and had osteoblastoma. *She would have died soon anyway.* She had a younger brother, aged three. Her dad was a useless drunkard while the mother worked in a cloth store striving hard to make money.

Oh, so she was the one with black glasses.

"Didn't you feel bad kidnapping the poor child? Snatching her away from her mother. The poor lady must be running hither and thither in search for her missing daughter," I said in a bold voice.

Everyone looked shocked again. It was quite evident that I was asking for death in that situation but I needed to know.

"You can't keep your mouth shut, can you?" He asked.

"You're right. I can't. Especially, for that level of brutality. You knew she was suffering from all that! Yet you troubled her for no reason! And now that she is somewhere six feet under the ground, her mother won't even know that she died by the gun of some stupid mental moron like you!"

Anechka aimed a gun at me.

"Know your place, Anechka," he said.

I saw Anechka's face go pale and shocked as of other "officers" , as well.

"A savior and an angel, aren't you sweetie?" He flashed a fake smile.

Putting my arms crossed to my chest, "Yes I am, you got any problem with that?" I returned the fake smile as well.

"Oof," he said getting up, cracking his neck and unbuttoning the one buttoned button of his suit.

I gulped.

Oh shit, I was in deep shit, wasn't I?

He grabbed me by my shirt and dragged me to the kitchen.

"I seriously need to put you in your place," he said.

My shirt was on the verge of tearing.

"Leave my shirt, you pervert!" I screamed while everyone still sat where they were. I was glad no one could see what was going on in the kitchen.

I wanted to bite his hand but I was scared to do so. I felt as if green gooey grasshopper blood would flow out if I bit him so I just kept pushing him away.

He pushed me to the kitchen counter. My headache had grown worse. But I could not let him get to me.

I was anguished and angry.

I walked up to him and pushed him hard. He was a lot tougher and stronger than I had imagined men would be.

He was around six feet or something, while I was five feet and two inches, which made me look inferior and weak, the feeling that I absolutely was repulsed by.

He smirked and held my hands and picked me up to his height.

"How about we complete some unfinished business of the last time?" He said getting closer to me.

I wanted to revolt to what he was doing but I felt a tingly feeling run down my spine, my heart racing faster.

I could not let that feeling take over me no matter how much I relished it, it was wrong.

I banged my head as hard as possible against his, making him gasp out in pain. I held his fake blonde hair and pulled out the wig revealing his bald head.

"You better let me go before I run out and show this to everyone." I threatened him.

"Go ahead," he said.

I knew I was failing miserably.

There was no way he was letting his grip around me loosen. I was squirming, trying hard to escape. I tried digging my nails which had grown from the passage of time, into his hands but I knew all I was digging into was the fake rubbery stuff that covered his real self.

He carried me to the nearby counter and pulled out a knife. I froze.

He is not going me to murder me, is he?

He placed the blade against my skin on the temple of my face and kept gazing at my face.

"Would not a scar decorate your face well, eh?" He said licking his lips.

I was shaking uncontrollably out of fear. I started thrashing around him.

"Let me go!" I yelled.

"Tsk tsk, moving around will make things worse sweetie," he said as he pulled down the gauze and dug the sharp edge of the knife into my skin.

It hurt a lot causing me to scream.

"Ah...now that was the scream I was hoping to listen." He said chuckling.

"You'll pay!" I sneered.

"Save your curses for later, lady, this is just the beginning. And you're not bold; you're weak like a chicken, helpless and pathetic. You could not even save that slutty friend of yours back there. You were sleeping while she was being abused and it was YOU who got her killed, you selfish bitch!" He said towering over me making me feel as small as possible.

We kept looking into each other's eyes for some time, the

transparent barrier of silence between us. For some reason, the silence did not make me feel uncomfortable. I was actually relieved that none of us were talking.

Tears were pooling in my eyes.

I am worthless, useless, always falling short of people's expectations.

Maybe that was why no one was friends with me. My forehead was burning from the scar that ran to my ears. Now people would call me uglier if I ever managed to see someone. No one would date me. There was no way I would have a life out of this. The police would send me to jail if they found out I was a murderer. I could never go back to my home and my family would not accept me.

But most of all, I felt guilty to have Mauni let go. It was my fault that I had proposed such horrifying idea to her. If I had not been that bold that night, and then maybe she would have been still breathing, dreaming to her fullest, trying her best to live what she wanted for.

I was responsible for the deaths of two people.

Maybe I did not regret killing the Aussie. But every deed has a reason behind it. Maybe he was really evil or maybe a sad lover whose woman must have left him to be like this. Sometimes, pain can blind a person to such an extent that they are not able to comprehend what is right or wrong for people those who are able to move on from that insanity to being sane have a really brave heart. But sometimes, the pain is so addictive that it's difficult to let go of it all.

But what happened with Mauni was all my fault. I could not forgive myself even if I could. I wanted to forget the past events but that was my weakness and my opponents would never fail to bring that up to bring me down.

He was already gone. Maybe back to the table. I wondered why he had not killed me already. What was holding him back?

I saw Anechka getting into the kitchen.

"Boss seeks you, join him on the table," that's all that she said.

I jumped from the counter and dragged my feet back to the seat, my hair disheveled and the sticky blood coating at one side of my face.

I pulled out my chair and sat on it like a queen, sprawling my legs on the table. I had no idea why I felt like it.

"Legs off the table," he said.

"And what if I don't take them off?" I asked looking at him.

"Utterly shameless, aren't you?"

"You sound like my class teacher from kindergarten," I said rolling my eyes, folding my hands across my chest.

He got up and moved to the corner of the room under the staircase, leading to the outside world. He pulled out a few ropes and went to the kitchen and came out with a duct tape.

"What in the world?" I said putting my legs down but I guess that was not appealing to the majesty.

He taped my waist so that I could not move while the rest of the scum squad kept looking.

I saw Baldie come forward.

"Shall we do it?" He asked.

"Back off, Boris," he said looking into my eyes. "You and Daniil have done enough."

I was kind of happy that I got to know their names and I had a mental friendship with Boris even if he behaved like an absolute prick to me.

I could feel ropes binding my legs to the chair. I groaned and before I could pull out his wig to reveal his true self, he held my wrists and taped me.

"Let me go!" I screamed again.

He held my neck in tight grip causing me to choke and shake violently.

"Shut your mouth!" He yelled at me.

"NO!" I yelled spitting on his face.

I felt a sharp pain on my cheek.

I looked at him with shock and disbelief.

"Did you just slap me?!" I yelled at him.

He got up, his arms on the arms of my chair. He started coming closer to me till the extent that our lips were almost touching. I squeezed my eyes and my lips shut tight and threw my head sideways. I definitely did not want to lose my precious kiss to a monster like him.

"Good," was all he said before taping my mouth, causing me to open my eyes in an instant.

"No! Hey!" I tried to say but the tape shut me out, muffling my helpless screams and tears streaming down my face. He got behind my chair and pushed it to its place.

"What a day," he said sighing.

I could see all the people looking at each other, clueless. They also looked a bit relieved.

He opened the file again.

Do we really have to do this?

"John Blake, an eight year old from Delaware. Parents own an auto dealership. What a pity they had to lose their pathetic excuse of a son."

Oh you are pathetic, you moron.

He looked at the other girl and smiled seductively at him, the same girl whom I had knocked out in the bathroom.

"Rebecca Nissan, oh darling, is not that you?"

She nodded like an eager puppy getting all giggly and excited. She legit looked like a crazier version of Harley Quinn.

And he was the Joker, of course.

Perfect couple~

I wanted to laugh. I thought that such kind of girls only existed in movies but oh boy, some people were indeed like that.

I saw him sliding his chair and patting his thighs lightly as if motioning her to sit on his lap.

She got up from her chair and got on his lap while his arms snaked around her waist while she clung on to him like a magnet.

I was mentally barfing and gagging.

EW, seriously?

"Rebecca Nissan, 19 and the most beautiful girl in the world," he said smiling at him while she smiled at him.

So, ladies and gentlemen, this is how people become the victims of Stockholm syndrome.

He was stroking her hair and went into details.

"Born in the United States but living in Dubai. Head cheerleader of the school and absolutely loves to be spoiled by rich things," he smiled.

"Oh yeah, daddy," she giggled.

I wanted to puke all over the place. Some things are better kept in private but this girl was going overboard.

"Then comes, Miss Yi Ling from Singapore."

She came from some village in Singapore.

She must have been around thirteen or so.

A shy girl who mostly kept quiet. She seemed like those kids who were easily targetted by the bullies. Her family had a ramen shop and she never went to school.

She was a pretty girl, though. She had bangs falling upon her eyes, porcelain white skin which looked as if they had been polished for the hundredth time. She had a few bruises here and there and a few nasty scars on her arms.

Poor kid.

"And now we have Mackenzie walker from Australia," he said looking at the curly, blonde haired girl at the far end of the desk. She looked furious and angry. Her princess-like beauty consisting of long flowing blonde hair, crystal blue eyes, clear skin, slender body, and long thin fingers were no match to how mad she looked at the moment. I bet she would snap at anyone at any moment now if there were no rules or terms and especially, the threat of death for every single wrongdoing.

"Mother and father, both are farmers. Has a grandfather who has leukemia and a little brother who now uses prosthetic legs just because of her carelessness. You quite remember the day when you pushed your brother in front of that car while you two were crossing the road after you bought him an ice cream, don't you?" He said.

That seemed utter nonsense. That could have been a mistake. Maybe she was too young and unfocused. I could see her hands clasped with each other really tight, so tight that I could see her knuckles through her skin, as if they would pop out that instant.

But then how did he know all of these minute details?

"Shandrel Dixon," he said looking at the agitated black boy whom I had tried to save earlier. His eyes had become red and he looked like a monster ready to lash out but yet again, he had to hold that all back in order to save himself.

"Sixteen and is from Jamaica. He does not have a father and his mother is a cook at weddings and mass food programmes. No wonder why you have that tier of fat around your waist," he said looking from his glasses and back to his book.

What a cocky idiot.

"Then comes, Edvin Engberg," I saw his eyes pointing to a chair near me, to the handsome green-eyed handsome hunk I was feeling jittery about once and then had pushed away from him due to his attitude.

"Nineteen, mom and dad who run a successful watch company. The one and only precious child. I wonder how they would feel if they found out that you were dead," he said showing him a mocking expression of pity.

I wondered where my introduction was.

"Now last but not the least, our darling miss, Asha Mohini."

There we go.

I wanted to correct him the way he was pronouncing my name but could not say anything since my mouth was taped shut. But anyway, he made it sound fancier and posh so I had no complaints.

He laid his sharp eyes on me and kept on describing me.

"Seventeen with a mother who is a senior executive officer and a father who is a senior bank manager and lives far away in the south, away from his family. I wonder what he does there in all those months when he is alone."

Now, what did he mean by that?

Hey! My dad stayed away from us so that he can work and send money to us. What the hell was he talking about?

And all this time that girl was clinging onto him like a monkey on a branch making everyone gag. I had seen many teen couples in my school holding hands and making out till they ran out of breath and this looked like a miniature version of it.

I muffle-screamed and shook my chair hard to get his attention.

"Oh look, somebody's jealous," he chuckled looking at her.

But before anything could happen he kissed her and they started making out. I shut my eyes close. I wanted to throw up. I could hear wet slick noises which violated me even more.

After a while, I felt a pair of cold hands detaching the tape off from my mouth and hands. He folded his legs with his hands on his knees and bent down to my height causing me to look away.

"Ew, take that filthy mouth away from me," I said.

That idiot leaned in closer, causing tears to well up in my eyes.

"Don't fall for me," was what he said.

I laughed.

"Fall for you? I wouldn't even if you were the last person on Earth," I snapped at him. I wanted to mention Daniel but I did not want to. This crazy man was capable of anything. I did not want him to reach out to him and do him any harm.

I saw a flash of hurt in his eyes.

Or maybe I thought it that way.

Wait...was it? It can't be...

"Good to know," he said getting back to his standing posture.

He grabbed her hands and started making way to the stairs while she followed giggling and laughing.

I shook my head, having a stretchy feeling around my mouth and where the tapes had been stuck. It must have had been the adhesive from the tape.

"And yes, as a punishment due to misconduct, you will be working in the kitchen and hallways."

We all sighed in relief when they went out while I sat there dumbstruck.

Anechka stepped forward.

"You will all be allowed to talk. Dinner is at eight and lunch at one. No one would be allowed to get out of the room except for Asha."

At least she could say my first name correctly.

Saying this, the group of ladies and men in uniform went to their usual hangout place which was the kitchen.

Edvin came to me and pat my back.

"At least you get to go out of this chamber," he said.

"Yeah..." I said trailing off, "Trying my best not to get killed."

He seemed less irritating than the last time.

Mackenzie seemed to be having trouble holding back her anger.

She stomped off her way to under the staircase where that moron had brought out the tape and the ropes from, and started throwing things here and there.

Two men, one of them Daniil, came running out to the room we were in and tried grabbing her.

She had turned very wild. She looked like Shiva with his third eye opened, going to perform the tandava and destroy the universe.

She seemed to have had become unmanageable. They were not being able to control her and that is when I saw Daniil pull out some kind of syringe from his pocket and without second thoughts, he stabbed her with it on her neck.

I saw her frame grow limp while they lifted her up and went up the stairs.

I was horrified at what had happened.

"Sh...she is alive...right?" I asked, clutching Edvin's hand tight looking up to him.

"Yeah, I think she is. That must have been a tranquilizer or some kind of anesthetic."

"Ooh, that's smart of you to make out. I thought she died or something."

"I was actually planning to join the med school but this

happened....." He said sadly.

"Oh...I'm sorry..." was all that I could manage to say.

He stood like that for a while and then bent down and untied the ropes which were holding my legs together.

I stood up.

"Thank you..." I said bowing down my head as I usually do in courtesy.

He laughed a bit and bowed extravagantly which made me laugh.

"That was quite a bow," I said laughing.

I had to be on good terms with everyone in order to not get into trouble.

Anechka got into the room.

"Follow me." She said.

I glanced briefly at Edvin and sighed following Anechka to the kitchen.

I heard a red-haired woman whistling when we got into the kitchen while the rest were chatting with each other in groups.

"Oooh, she is the one he favors so much," she said smiling kindly at me.

She was the first lady I received positive vibes from.

Anechka pulled out a white garment from a stack of similar garments out of a drawer and handed me one.

I unfolded it and found out that it was actually a really short white dress which looked like a maid uniform.

Without getting bothered by the words of the red-haired lady, she asked me to try it on, leading me to a walk-in refrigerator as there was no other space.

I changed there and came out trying to pull down the skirt a little more.

"Um...this is too short...can I get a longer one, please?" I said frowning.

I was not habitual of wearing dresses at all, let alone the short ones as this.

"You look sexaaaaay in that dress, gal!" The red-haired lady said.

"Cut it out, Dasha." Anechka said. "You're being too kind," she said going through another drawer pulling out an apron looking longer than my dress, which I was grateful for.

"And you're being too harsh," she said looking grave.

Dasha jumped off the counter and snatched the apron away from her hands flashing her white teeth at me, and handed that to me while I looked at her like a mute calf.

"Cheer up!" She said shaking me playfully.

I kept on staring at her like that.

She kneeled to me.

"I know it's not that easy but you should always smile, even during the tough times," while Anechka stood behind her, rolling her eyes.

"Are you two done with your mom-daughter talk?" She asked.

She looked down for a moment lost in some kind of deep thought for a second and looked up at me again, smiling.

"I guess," she said smiling wide again.

I put on the apron and Anechka walked out.

I knew I had to follow her. I looked back at Dasha again. She waved at me with quick hand sways and I could not help but smile and wave back before continuing following her.

I followed her the same way we had taken earlier and got out of the walk-in fridge. I saw the old woman and the younger girl in the kitchen.

"Diana, I'm leaving her to you for the work as boss had said. Converse with her in English. She cannot speak Russian," Anechka said and exited the room out of the kitchen.

I looked back at the old woman.

She was wearing a yellow colored short midi frock with a pearl necklace while a faint pink lipstick adorned her barely visible shrunken lips. It looked as if she was getting ready for some old ladies' get together or a kitty party, except that she had her apron on.

"This is Alyosha," she said pointing to the younger girl who had smiled at me earlier.

She looked up at me from chopping the celery and smiled at me and I smiled back at her.

“Do you know how to cook or any basic skills about cooking?” She asked.

“I don’t think I do but I can do a few things,” I replied feeling unsure about every word I said.

“How about you show me your chopping skills?” She asked flipping the knife high up in the air and catching it with the handle with ease while her other hand rested on her waist making me gasp.

She looked like an expert chef, a strand of her auburn hair falling in front of her eyes while her frail body was clad in a white frock and white apron. She looked like some young farmer’s wife, an expert in cooking stuff.

“Don’t do that, it’s dangerous,” I said to her.

“No, it’s not, it’s fun,” she said laughing softly and doing it again.

“Oh jeez,” I said making a face.

She laughed yet again.

“Come on over here,” she said motioning me to come to her.

I walked to her and she handed me a knife which made me nervous. She gave me an onion. My hands shook uncontrollably while trying to cut it. Needless to say, my hands trembled really badly and I ended up cutting my finger.

“Hey! Be careful!” She said rummaging through the drawer and pulling out a band-aid. She opened the kitchen tap and placed my hand under the flowing water. She wiped it off with a clean kitchen towel, finally wrapping my finger with the sticky band-aid.

“This is what happens when you ask a girl to cut vegetables when all she has ever cooked is instant noodles,” I said laughing softly.

“You want to work or rest? It looks like a pretty deep cut,” she asked taking a curious look at my finger.

"I can help with little things. Besides, I don't want to get killed by that grumpy monster," I said and we both erupted in fits of laughter.

"You both will get into trouble if he listens to you," Diana said with worry evident in her voice. She was tasting some kind of broth or soup. "When will you learn to season the food correctly, Alyosha?" She said with annoyance.

"Now what's wrong with that soup, Granny?" She said making her way to the counter where the soup was boiling.

Oh, she was her grandma.

She took some in a ladle, blew it a little to lessen down the heat maybe and sipped some, instantly spitting it all out.

"Oh God, that is so salty!" She said her face still scrunched with disgust.

"How much time do you have before you serve?" I asked.

"Forty or fifty minutes," She said her face struck with panic.

I raised an eyebrow.

"And is everything prepared?" I asked.

"He only eats soup and bread for lunch," She said. "And he always eats those slow cooked soups," she groaned. "Those take such a long time to be made and are so difficult to make."

"Fancy, I see," I said.

"Well, he eats nothing else so..." Diana said almost defending him.

"Okay...let me see if I can do something." I said.

"You said all you cook is instant noodles," she said mockingly.

"Well, I know what I'm doing." I retorted.

I knew that soup had become horrible. From the kind of face that she had made, I did not even want to taste that liquid.

"If he does not like his food this time, he will fire us," Diana said scared.

"I don't think he will fire you, I know he will shoot each one of us," I said.

"We have to try something different better and quick," I stated.

"I'm clueless, he never likes our food," she said clutching her hair.

I saw a packet of fettuccini pasta on the top shelf.

"Get me that packet of pasta, please," I asked her.

"I told you, he only eats bread and soup. He will kill us if we cook anything else!" She shouted.

"Jeez, you talk too much," I said shaking my head. "Just get me that thing if you want to keep your job!" I raised my voice.

"Just do it," Diana said.

She glared at Diana.

I shook my head and went to the pantry and luckily found it near the rice.

I ran over and emptied the packet of pasta in that salty broth while I asked her to cut me some avocados, lettuce, Roma tomatoes, and red onions.

I saw her knife cutting through the vegetables as fast as lightning. I had to admit that she had awesome chopping skills. I was surprised when Diana put a bottle of extra virgin olive oil on the counter next to me.

"Italian is good," she said.

I prepared a cheese sauce and put my strained soup flavored pasta in the sauce. Diana tasted it.

"It's pretty decent," she said.

I was mentally dissatisfied with the remark but at least it was a lot better than salt flavored soup and bland bread.

Cheese makes everyone happy, almost everyone.

I assembled the croutons, the lettuce and the other salad vegetables and Diana poured the salad dressing that she had been preparing while I finished it off with a drizzle of the olive oil.

"What about dessert?" I asked getting nervous.

"He does not eat sweet," Diana said.

"Oh....." I said wondering why.

"Yeah, else how would he be able to keep his bitter attitude intact?" Alyosha said.

I giggled a little.

"True," I agreed.

"It's time for the show," Alyosha said glancing at the kitchen clock.

She tugged out her apron and threw it carelessly on the kitchen counter. She pulled out a trolley that I had seen the servers serve the food on in hotel rooms in the big restaurants and carefully placed the food condiments on them with a flower vase and a glass jug with ice cold water and a few slices of lemon in it.

"Wow.....he is some kind of royalty or what?" I laughed.

"You bet he thinks he is," she said laughing as well pushing the food trolley out with her.

"Can I come along with you?" I asked following her.

"You better clean the hallways, Anechka told me you had to work in the hallways too, specifically cleaning. I hope he does not kill me for altering his special menu."

"Ugh...okay..." I mumbled, "But where are the cleaning equipments?" I asked.

"Third room at your right when you're out of the kitchen," Diana said.

I saw Alyosha vanish to the left of the kitchen.

"Thank you," I said.

She smiled.

"I have never seen Fyodor so enthusiastic before this," she said.

"Fyodor?...Fyodor, who?" I asked confused.

"Boss." was all she said.

Oh...that monster has a name.

Diana sat in a huge wooden chair.

"I bet he is always over enthusiastic doing atrocious acts of brutality and stupidity," I said. "Besides he has a girlfriend. Love at first sight. Perfect!" I said rolling my eyes.

She laughed.

"She will not last for long," she said.

That made me nervous.

"Um...what?" I asked to recheck if what I heard and was thinking did match.

"You will see. And you should hurry up. He does not like unpunctual people," she said sternly.

I just nodded and made my way to the cleaning room.

I entered the room and looked around the room. There was a huge window and I could see the blue sky and the green grassy carpets across the field.

I sighed.

I wished if I could free the rusty hooks of the window and open it to let fresh air come in but they were too tight to open. It felt as if they had not been opened since they were probably made. I was not foolish enough to try out things with a futile outcome since I had other important works to attend to.

I picked up the mopping bucket and the mop, the broom and the plastic feather duster and a cloth. I was glad that the mopping bucket had slots to hold it all in. Seeing an extra slot empty, I filled it with a bottle which had a blue liquid but without any label. I was pretty sure it was some stuff like *cleanex* or something as it smelled like it.

I filled the bucket with water from a tap in the corner of the room. It seemed like each and every room was planned to serve a particular purpose. No room would ever have a tap below the sink level just like that. I pulled the mopping bucket out of the room and carefully shut it behind, switching off the lights.

I swept, dusted and cleaned the entire floor and dragged my bucket to the top with difficulty. Something about the upper floor made me nervous.

Wait, I've been here before, have I not? The last room with the ebony door was enough to refresh my memory.

I went to the far end of the hallway, opposite to where the room was.

I started cleaning as slowly as possible in order to avoid confronting that door. I was scared he would burst out of that door and something stupid would happen.

Time passed by and I heard weird noises coming out from behind that door. They sounded more like…moans? I could not help but get disgusted by that.

So that was what was going on.

That was when the handle of my mop slipped through my slippery soapy hands and hit the door.

Oh shit!

And that's when all the sounds stopped.

I scurried my frame to the middle of the hallway, red with embarrassment when the door opened.

Oh God I'm so dead.

"Oh, so it's you," he said which made me stop dead in my tracks. "Someone is really curious."

I was mentally praying that he did not kill me for interrupting him.

"Um…y…yes, Mr. Fyodor," I squeaked. "Sorry the mop slipped, I didn't mean to pry or anything."

Holy moly, someone please kill me.

I wanted to murder myself for speaking out his name.

He lifted my chin up with his index to face him while I stood there like a good girl, not ignoring the trembling part.

"How do you know my name?" He asked looking at me suspiciously.

"I heard it from the kitchen."

"Enough of talking. Join our little party," he offered.

"No thanks, please," I said getting away from him.

"That was an order, not an offer," he said gripping me tightly by my arm and dragging me into the room.

I was greeted by the familiar curtains and the glass windows but this time, they closed behind the unfolded curtains and on the bed was none other than Rebecca. She had clad herself in sheets, her hair all messy, while their clothes were in a careless pile somewhere near the bed. There was a bucket of half melted ice and glasses of unfinished red wine lying on the table near the bed.

"Um...terribly sorry to disrupt your moment, but can I go?" I asked politely.

"Go where?..." He asked snaking his arms around me. I could feel his soft fluffy bathrobe against my bare arms and my back against his chest while he rested his face in the crook of my neck sending tingly sparks running all over my body.

I started to panic.

"Let me go!" I said writhing within his strong grip.

"Not that easily," he said placing his rough chapped lips against the skin of my neck.

"The hell!" I said trying my best to pry his hands away from me.

I looked at Rebecca. There was a look of anger and jealousy on her face. In a flash, she pulled out a gun and aimed at me.

Was this some kind of sick joke?

I was not ready to give in yet just because of her anger.

I felt something cold against my jaw realizing a bit later that it was a gun too.

"Sick lovers obsessed with blood," I said rolling my eyes, quitting shortly after trying my hardest as I knew it would be futile for me to break from his grip. Needless to say, I had grown frustrated by these people having their way with me. Even if I had not been able to fight until then, I was willing to give it a shot.

I banged my head against his head causing him to loosen his grip around me. I was scared that he had a gun but maybe my adrenaline rush did not permit to see through the dangerous sides of the situation. I lashed out on her.

Who did she think she was?

Who gave her the right to be that way to me?

I pinned her down on the bed twisting her arm in a harsh manner which caused her to yelp and let go of the gun causing me to snatch that and aim at her, holding her arms tightly behind her back. There were only three words to describe her; weak, defenseless and pathetic. I grabbed her hands and kneeled behind her, my knees making deep craters on the soft mattress. The bed in my house did not have a fluffy mattress so this felt good, something I would find in a hotel room. I wanted to plop down on that and fall asleep. I wanted to slap myself for even thinking about something like that in such a situation.

I saw him chuckling in the darkness of the room, the feeble green lamp on the nightstand glowing at its hardest it seemed, trying to illuminate the room with its light.

"One more step and I'm blowing her," I threatened.

"Oh honey, do me the honor please," he smirked causing Rebecca to gasp leaving my head in a jumbled mess of thoughts when Diana's words played in my mind.

Even if I was confused I was not foolish to let go of her hands that easily.

"Too weak," he said drawing closer making my frame shiver.

Something in his words intimidated me, made my heart beat fast, and gave me mixed feelings of fear, nervousness and something else that I could not bring myself to.

Before I could think even a single thing more, I heard a loud bang which left my ears ringing for a while causing me to jump back as the dead body of the girl fell limp on my arms.

I saw blood seeping into my clothes. Unable to bear it, I pushed the body aside looking at him in shock and horror.

"Why would you even do that?" I asked, raising my voice a little.

He rolled his eyes, his wire-framed teeth peeking from his mouth.

"Don't be such a novice," he said. "You're secretly happy that she is gone, aren't you?"

"You're bonkers to even think of such a possibility! I mean, I sure hated her but...you two had a thing I guess?"

"Mhm.....you were jealous? Weren't you?" He said drawing closer to me.

"Why would I be jealous?" I asked him shrugging and shrinking back from him.

"Coz I am hot and irresistible," he said smirking.

"Yeah, behind all that prosthetic makeup," I said with clear sarcasm lacing my voice.

He kept silent and so did I.

I knew I had struck a nerve.

As evil as I thought he was, it was a devilish act on my behalf. Even if he was horrible to me, I could not bear to hurt him this way. I grew up with body consciousness issues myself, the fat deposit on my lower abdomen hardly helping with my situation. Shaming could be quite degrading. It brought down one's self-esteem to level zero, and I did not want anybody to go through that, not even him. The poor fellow had to live like this his entire life and I knew it was not funny. I actually thought that apologizing to him would be a weak move, but I also knew that good things never exhibited weakness.

"Everyone is beautiful just the way they are. You realize that was just a joke, right?"

"Oh, so now you find me beautiful?" He said smiling cockily and plopping down on the bed next to me.

I sighed and turned to walk out of the room shaking my head. I turned back and looked at him. It seemed as if he was playing with the dead body's hair.

Disgusted by this habit of his I yelled, "Are you necrophilic or something?"

Maybe that did not bother him.

A month ago or something, I would have puked all over, seeing that but now, death, blood, and flesh hardly fazed me.

I was out of my rational mindset for sure. You could not be normal when so many abnormal switches came to your life. He was smiling and cuddling at the sheets when my curious self went back to him and shook him hard.

"Are you a necrophilic or what?" I repeated causing his eyes to open wide and look at me.

The next thing I knew that he had pulled me on top of him causing me to gasp. The setting was perfect. I was lying on a living monster who barely had anything on with a pale, bloody and smelly body next to us.

"The hell, what you're doing?" I screeched.

He looked up at me and smiled; a genuine one. He looked so beautiful. Why could he not be like this all the time? Smiling and cheerful. I could not see much in that darkness but there was this sheen of radiance and for once I felt a positive aura and happiness despite of all the negativity around us.

Or wait, this could be a trap. He knew what people loved and wanted and used it against them. This may be my end, without my own knowledge.

I banged my head against him causing him to gasp in pain.

He was rubbing his head when I pulled away, a clear expression of pain on his face.

"You're lucky I don't have a strong skull," he said still whining and rubbing his head.

"Get someone to get rid of this body, now will you?" I said not paying attention to him, more focused on what should have been done.

"Oui, mademoiselle," he said in a French accent which sounded as good as the original, making my eyes widen and him to chuckle.

He grabbed his phone from his nightstand and called someone speaking in Russian. Even if I could not understand a word of what he said, I saw his face going stone hard and cold. That made me kind of sad. What could compel a person so much that they would change themselves from being warm to that of cold like this? I mean, I had my problems but I tried to be funny and not take much by heart. Something really must have had happened.

I saw some people get inside the room and take the body away. It had already begun to stench causing me to flinch and my clothes had started to smell.

I got out of the room while they were busy doing stuff. I was in the mid hallway when I felt a hand around my shoulder.

To be honest, he being like this around me made me feel uncomfortable. I was not used to such attention, love, and care.

I swatted his hands away.

"What?" He asked surprised.

I stopped and looked up at him.

"Why are you being like this?" I asked him in an irritated voice.

"What do you mean," he asked taken aback.

"Why do you treat me differently?" I asked him raising my voice.

"You think you're special so I treat you differently?" He asked in a stern voice.

"Why didn't you kill me when I was against your rules? Huh? Tell me!" I asked yelling.

I knew he was tongue tied. He did not know the answer but maybe he did and did not want to say.

I stared at him for a while and walked off to the kitchen. I remember leaving the cleaning the equipment behind. I peeked from behind the kitchen door to find out that he was still standing there. I roamed about the kitchen for around seven minutes and checked again. I was relieved to find out that he wasn't there. I strutted my way to the end of the hallway and panicked to find out that the equipment was not where I had kept before. I checked at spots all around the hallway. I could not misplace things.

Would they kill me for misplacing such a silly thing as this?

Where could an entire set of mop and basket go?

Maybe the workers who had come in for cleaning kept it in the place where it should have been kept?

I walked to the cleaning room to find that the door was left ajar. I almost let out a yelp to find Fyodor in there with the equipment that I had left. I rushed to him taking it from his hands.

"Now what happened?" He said lifting up the cleaning product higher while I kept jumping all around him to give that back to me.

"I need to keep that in its right place, damn it!" I said still jumping around.

"What's wrong with me keeping it?" He asked.

I sighed. He was the owner of the house and I was the maid. Or maybe my mind was convinced that a guy having a real idiotic behavior as him was too stupid to understand that or even do it. Helping around the lower authorities, I meant.

I stood there and put out my hand.

"Give that to me. Right Now," I said sternly.

"I won't," he said and kept them all at the top and walked away while I kept staring at them on the top like an idiot fellow.

Maybe I'll see about that tomorrow.

I thought and closed the door and walked to the kitchen refrigerator.

Luckily I was on time and found Anechka waiting in the kitchen.

"What is this?" She escaped looking down at my bloody uniform.

"What did you do?" She said slapping me hard causing tears to well up in my eyes.

"He killed Rebecca, not me! It's not my fault that he dragged me into it." I yelled as loudly as possible.

I rubbed my cheek at the sudden slap. God, it did hurt badly. It felt like a bone frame hitting my face.

I saw her eyes widened, looking at behind me. Before I could look behind me, there was a gunshot and the next thing I knew, it was blood on my face, well not a whole lot but sure there were a few splatters of it. I looked behind me instantly. And there he was in his bloody robe, and now he had killed another woman, this time someone who was known to be very close to him.

He walked to me and opened the fridge and opened the cell inside it using the biometric device at the door. He looked dead serious and I knew it was best to shut up. I scurried along the opening. Luckily, the door to the basement was open. I came down.

Everyone there looked at me horrified.

All the other gang members looked shocked. I saw Daniil coming in.

"Put her to rest," he said. "Boss's orders."

"Where's Anechka?" Dasha asked.

"She is dead," he replied bluntly.

There was a lot of whispering.

Dasha took me to the nearby room and opened the room with a key.

I saw everyone.

Everyone was laughing and talking. Most probably, mingling and trying to get to know each other despite the differences and the situation we were in. I was trying to be as resilient and oblivious to the situation as I could. I walked in and the room fell silent.

"Hi," Edvin said which caused me to smile and say everyone "hi" back.

They looked at me with pure shock and horror. Maybe from the blood on my face and clothes.

The first thing I knew, I had to go to the bathroom.

I showered and got out. There was a rack with my name on it. I opened it and found my bag in it. I pulled out fresh clothes and came out and climbed on the upper bunker, deciding to join them.

Death

“Well, hello,” Yi Ling said when I got to the bed.

“Hi,” I said timidly.

“Hey, how do you know English when you never went to school?” I asked her surprised.

“My oomi taught me,” she said smiling.

“Oomi?...” I asked her cluelessly.

“My mother…pardon me,” she apologized.

“Oh, it’s alright,” I said smiling.

I used to call my mom ‘maaun’ anyways, so I understood.

“Rebecca is dead,” Emerico said.

“That slut deserved it anyway,” Shandrel joined.

“Why was there blood on your clothes?” Ying asked.

“I helped in lifting up her body when it was taken away,” I lied again.

For some reason leaking official information seemed too risky. I had to survive.

“Mackenzie is out of the radar too,” Edvin said while the others agreed.

“What?! why?! What did she do?” I asked shocked.

“Unfit for experiment,” Edvin said. “She had some mental issues. Also damn unmanageable”

“Where did you get this information from?”

“We overheard two of them talking,” Edvin replied.

"I'm heading to bed," Shandrel said yawning.

I felt my stomach growl, perhaps it was so loud that everyone stopped and looked at me.

"Oh, you need to get the dinner, you missed it," Emerico said.

I sighed.

Getting down from the bunker bed, I banged on the door. They opened after the hundredth time it seemed. I was sleepy and tired yet hungry.

Dasha opened the door.

"Anything you need, sweetie?" She asked.

"I'm hungry," I whined.

She patted her head making a tsking noise.

"I can be so forgetful at times. Follow me," she said.

I followed her to the basement kitchen to find that no one was there.

"Where is everyone?" I asked.

"Bedtime, honey," she replied serving me bread, some kind of soup and sausages.

"Um...I don't eat red meat so, can you take this away from me please?" I asked politely, pushing away the sausage plate.

"Oh, are you a Hindu too?" She asked me delightedly.

"Yes," I looked at her with shock and awe.

"Rakesh was a Hindu too," she said smiling.

"Rakesh?" I asked almost trying to supress how funny the name sounded when she said it.

"My husband," she said.

"Oh does he work here too?" I asked feeling happy to have found an Indian person I could meet or talk to maybe.

"Oh, um…they passed away," she said, the glassy eyes and the unspoken pain clearly spoke what she really felt within.

"They?..." I stopped eating.

"My newborn kid and him. They were murdered," she said getting up and going away.

"Wait," I asked her to wait and tell me everything.

"What happened? Care to say?" I asked. "But you don't have to if you don't want," I said playing with my soup, all my hunger gone from listening to this.

"Let's say they punished me because I did something I should not have done," she said.

"But who killed them?" I asked.

"Boss and I'm still here paying off my debts," she said. "I should not be stressing you out than you already are," she informed.

How could he be that insensitive to kill a child?

This place was full of mysteries.

I finished my food and she led me to the room again.

"Sleep well," she said smiling.

"You too," I said.

The lights were off. There were small red night-bulbs glowing. Everyone was sleeping.

I carefully climbed on the bunker bed to the top where I earlier was and got inside the covers. Unable to comprehend what I had experienced the entire day, I was fast asleep.

I woke up to the blaring of a siren system, panicked. Everyone had woken up too.

"The hell was that!" Edvin exclaimed.

Dasha opened the door.

"You have fifteen minutes to get ready," he informed in a stern voice.

We all ran hither tither to get ready. As difficult it was, we managed to do it and within an hour and thirty minutes, we were at the breakfast table.

"Asha, you will have to go for work now and the rest of you all will follow me," she said.

This was a whole new side of hers. It seemed as if she was trying to be...Anechka?

Why can't people be just the way they were?

I put my uniform and waited for Dasha to open the biometric secured lock.

"Your fingerprints have been entered in the lock system. You can open the necessary facilities yourself," she said.

I was surprised to hear that.

"Don't stand there gawking. He won't like it if you're late," she said.

I made my way to the kitchen, copying the steps how the others used to do while escorting me.

"Well, hello there, Asha," Diana said knitting a yellow scarf.

"Hello, and good morning," I said cheerfully.

Alyosha walked to me and hugged me while I hugged her back, "There's a piece of awesome news," she said.

"What is that?" I asked her being all excited.

"For the first time in his life is he eating breakfast and actually he is eating the same pasta that you cooked for yesterday's lunch."

I could not believe.

"What? You can't be serious," I said. "He really likes eating crazy food then."

"Well, that's what happened so, I'm heating the leftovers. Besides he is going easy on people here. Never has that ever happened," she said.

"That poor boy is growing soft," Diana said looking at her knitting items from the brink of her glasses.

I laughed.

"Soft? He killed two people yesterday," I mocked.

"He used to kill five each day," Alyosha said.

"Why can't the cops take him away?" I asked.

"He bribes them and besides, he has extremely loyal people who wouldn't even budge for ransom," she said.

"Now, that's some serious loyalty," I said.

"I know."

I went to the other corner of the kitchen drawer and pulled out my apron.

I was surprised to see that there was an array of pancakes,

crepes, sausages, ham, and tomatoes.

"Hey, Alyosha!" I called out to her.

She came to me. "What?" She asked.

I pointed to a plate of crepes with strawberry and whipped cream.

"I thought he doesn't eat sweet," I asked.

"Those are for the others," she informed. "Besides, it's your turn to serve him breakfast today," she said.

"What? Why?" I asked being scared and shocked.

"He said so."

"Oh lord no," I said.

"Oh lord yes," she said. She held my hands and dragged me to the microwave.

She pulled out the dish, served it on the plate and told me to go to the room on the far left of the kitchen, at the end.

I walked holding the plate of pasta and entered the room.

There were lots of people eating there, all of them wearing black uniforms.

Certain men snickered while watching me look around helpless, searching for the main person.

I saw him chatting away with some old guy at the end of a table.

I walked to him sneering at the laughing men.

"Oh, here you are!" He said. "Well, good morning, hun?" He said smiling which almost looked fake.

I smiled back and placed the plate on his table and he started drowning in his food, gobbling up everything like a hungry cat.

The room dropped dead silent.

I looked around to find that everyone had stopped to look at him. There were even people who had their fork halfway to their mouth but had stopped right there, all of their eyes fixed on him.

I had my hands entwined with each other, in a standing posture like that of a good and obedient servant and stared at everyone in surprise while they watched him eat.

What was so strange in him eating? I mean, he was just eating. He looked at everyone, gulping down his bolus.

"What? Eat!" He bellowed causing everyone to go back to eating.

"Oh gosh! He is eating pasta for breakfast!" A young lady squealed who sat a few chairs away.

The blonde bimbo next to her was like, "Leave alone the breakfast! He is eating! What is in that food?" She asked curiously eyeing at the plate and then to me causing me to look away.

He finished his plate and wiped off his mouth with his napkin cloth and put it on the table while I waited for him to dismiss me. I had learned a thing or two on how to act like a maid and stuff which was helping me then and for which I could not have been more grateful.

"You should eat carefully, master," the old man next to him said.

"I was hungry," he said monotonously.

"How come you are eating breakfast today?" He asked.

"New recruitment in the kitchen," was all he answered looking down at his empty plate.

"Would you like some more, sir?" I asked politely, my insides screaming to how I had to behave. It was all yin and yang with my physical and mental state.

"I'm good," he said smiling at me professionally to which I got confused on how to react. So I just did my usual little bow and was going away when he grabbed my hand causing me to freeze in my spot. There were indeed a few people who were quite astonished on how he had been reacting lately.

"Stay," he said.

I could see a range of emotions there just like the levels of acidity and basicity on a pH scale. Some looked shocked, some were just frozen while some sat there looking at everything dreamily. I am sure I had heard some 'oohs' and 'aahs' and 'awws' while the rest minded their own business. He was doing something that I hated the most, that is attracting attention.

Seriously? You had to pull that stunt?

I looked back trying to look all innocent and flushed but inside I felt like hitting his skull with the cast iron skillet on which Alyosha seared the steak.

"Yes, sir?" I squeaked looking at him.

I had a zero experience being a maid but I did know that this was not the way owners were supposed to behave with them. He glared at a guy who sat on his left side causing him to gather his plate and move somewhere else.

I gave him a "what the hell?" look to which he pulled the chair for me to sit.

I kept standing there unsure if I should sit or not.

"What are you looking at? Sit," he said firmly.

"Maids are not supposed to sit with their masters?" I said, rather questioning him.

"We are not in the Elizabethan era so you can chill," he said.

"It's still not proper," I retorted.

He rolled his eyes keeping quiet for a moment, facepalming; the sound of the cluttering cutlery, shuffling of feet and the indistinct talking of a language I could make no sense out of.

He gave me a sardonic smile which made me wonder for what he had in his mind.

"You better sit down if you don't want your friend, Edvin dead," he said.

I was tired enough to deal with it. It would be a huge wastage of time to argue with him. So instead of blabbering with him like a bunch of immature kids, I sat my butt down on the chair. He pulled out a plate of pancakes and put it in front of me.

"Eat," he said.

It was not fair. Other people in maid uniforms were working their asses off while I was sitting there eating.

"This is not good what you're doing," I stated.

"Just do what I said," he said.

"I can't sit here and eat while the other employees of my rank are working hard. It's better if I go back to the kitchen and help my fellow cook to work and it's not Edvin's fault so please don't involve him in here," I said getting up feeling bad and avoiding the whole situation.

"It was nice meeting you, sir," I said bowing to the old man and then Fyodor and walking out maintaining my composure.

"What took you so long?" Alyosha asked. I could feel a tinge of annoyance in her voice.

He made me sit and asked me to eat with him.

She looked at me shocked.

"What?" She asked bewildered. "Tell me you didn't!" She exclaimed.

"I did sit on the chair after a bit of persuasion but then I reasoned and came out. It felt weird and horrible," I said.

"Thankfully, you passed the employee test," Diana said putting in some kind of bread dough in the oven.

"What is that?" I strolled to her.

"Sourdough," she answered.

"And what is this employee test?" I asked.

"He tests his employees," she said. "He likes everything to be organised and disciplined, even if things are going very lenient these days, I wonder why. He is often lost in thoughts and hardly pays attention to things."

"He needs to snap out of his dreams then. Also the consequences of the failures are?" I asked curiously.

"Acid bath," she said calmly.

"What? Anyone can die from an acid bath!" I asked shocked. This guy had to be mad.

"That's the point," Alyosha said making my head turn to her.

The day in the kitchen was oddly silent.

After a few hours of me working in the kitchen, Alyosha told me to go back to the basement.

"But why? It isn't time for me to go yet," I asked.

"Dasha had informed me to send you earlier. Master's orders," she said.

I remembered what Dasha had told the others. I smelt trouble in the air, the vibe of death around me. I took out the apron which clung to my body and kept it in the kitchen drawer. It felt as if something was missing. Alyosha looked distant and lost in her thoughts. Her bubbly and cheerful self was missing.

I kept a hand on her shoulder and squeezed a little in order to provide her comfort.

"Is everything alright?" I asked her softly.

"Yes…" she said quietly.

"You sure?" I asked her.

She was avoiding looking me in the eye. I knew something was wrong.

"Look at me," I said to her pulling her arms to face me.

There were tears welled up at the lower rim of her eyes, threatening to spill out.

"Heeeeeeey, why you're crying?" I cooed.

"Nothing.....just remembered something. Besides, you should get going. You're getting late. There will be consequences," she said nudging me half-heartedly.

"You should hurry," Diana said agreeing.

I dragged my feet to my way there, Alyosha's tearful eyes in my mind.

My mind was constantly wondering why she was like that? What was she thinking?

What›s going on?

I entered the basement to find five pairs of eyes trained at me, disappointment evident on their faces.

"Work, I apologize," I said going to sit at my place around the table.

I saw that there were a few syringes and cotton swabs and a small metal case.

"What..... is this?" I asked doubtfully.

Shandrel had gone pale. Edvin was sweating while Yi Ling

kept clutching to him. I was unsure what was going to happen. If given a chance, I would have run away. I looked at Fyodor who had his eyes trained on the metal box. He must have been an expert in masking his emotions for I could see none of them. Dasha looked emotionless as well.

"Your turn first, Asha," Fyodor said getting up.

I knew I had to follow him so I did.

We got out of the room and to the kitchen. I was surprised to find that the kitchen was empty.

"Where's everyone in the kitchen?" I asked my heart beating fast.

"Sent back to their rooms," he said being straightforward.

He took me out of the kitchen, holding my hands squeezing it lightly as if to give me comfort which confused me a lot.

He took me across the hallways I had no idea existed. He unlocked a room which was dark inside. He went inside first while I stood outside peeking into the room.

"Come on in," he said in a deep grave voice.

I was unsure.

"I can't see anything," I said.

"Just walk in," he said.

This was the calmest way he had ever spoken to me. I had a bad feeling at the pit of my stomach. But yet, strangely, his words comforted me.

I walked in, only the lighted doorway visible. My body twitched in fear when the door banged shut. I was too scared to speak. I was breathing heavily, so heavily that I bet he could hear that too.

"Ease down," he said.

I was wondering what was happening. It couldn't be one of his experiments now, would it?

"You're testing something on me, aren't you?"

"True," he said.

I was not mentally prepared for it.

"B...but I'm not ready," I said.

"There is a reason you were not informed," he said darkly near my ears sending chills to my spine.

His strangely warm hands held mine as he led me to sit on a single chair.

My heart was thumping hard.

"Get ready," he whispered taking both of my hands behind the chair and handcuffing me making me gasp.

I had grown nauseous and neither his voice nor the cold metal against my wrist was helping me to calm me down.

I could hear his footsteps moving far away from me.

Is he leaving me?

"Don't leave me alone," I whispered.

I got no answer, tears already spilling from my eyes.

Conducting simple scripted experiments in the science lab was enough to freak the hell out of me. How was I supposed to deal with this? What would happen to me? Would I lose an organ? Would I turn into something different? What if it fails?

This could be death...

A screen illuminated in front of me. I looked behind me to the top where there was a projector.

We were seeing some movie?

I looked down and yelped to find his face extremely close to me. The light from the screen was the only source of light for me to see my surroundings. But unfortunately, I could see nothing except a bit of myself and his face.

"Calm down," he said.

I felt something sharp being penetrated into my arm.

"What is it?" I asked panicking hard.

"Something I've been preparing for a very long time," he said turning my face forcefully to the screen.

I felt as if some kind of toxin was injected in me; the area I was injected in still burnt hard. As far from my experience with injections, they never hurt after a few minutes but this was getting worse, the pain increasing each passing second.

I stared at the screen. It seemed to be a CCTV footage. Then it turned out to be some kind of movie.

A film of a girl played. There was a nude explicit, censored scene. She seemed like some kind of stripper in a dance club, maybe an escort. There's a blur next. Then it seemed like there was a man in her life. Maybe she falls in love and they married. The next thing I see is a little girl with pigtails.

Wheat fields.

The couple is walking with their hands entwined and gazing into each other's eyes. And then there's a kiss. My mind was convinced that it was a happy ending which kinda made me smile. Then I felt dizzy. I saw a blur of colors. The next thing I see is a car moving on a rainy night- The same woman from the movie calling someone over the phone. She seemed in a hurry while the same little girl trailed after her dragging a big stuffed bunny, with one of her hands clutched on her mother's skirt.

The next scene I saw was that of the door banging. The woman's face lost color. She held her child close to her and within moments she started for the basement. There's this blur again. And this time, there is some kind of pain in my head. The pain starts growing and out of nowhere, I realize that I had my eyes closed this entire time. There is this huge migraine in my head. Then there is another burst of color and I see the woman hiding among some boxes in a basement, holding her hands on her daughter's mouth.

The migraine was getting worse.

I wanted the expanding migraine to stop but I also wanted to know what would happen next. I had a feeling that everything would stop with the migraine so I kept going.

The woman was pulled out of her hiding place by her hair, her face contorting in pain. Everything I was seeing was in a hue of red and black.

There were several men who also ripped the child out of the mother's arms. I could see the child screaming. It was as if I was deaf and mute. It felt so real. I wanted to do something. It felt as if I was there the entire time but could do nothing. I was trying to hit the men but it all went as if I was non-existent.

Frustration got the best of me when that happened. They shot the kid right in her head while her mother was in tears yelling and screaming when they held her. I screamed, my helpless and powerless voice so loud yet not affecting them a bit which angered me even more. The next thing I knew was body pain in different parts of the body, more on my hands and head, basically in knuckles. It felt as if somebody was tearing my skin and flesh apart which made me scream even more. I saw the woman being shot. The headache got at its worst which made me scream endlessly. Then what I see is the husband and father. It looked as if he had tried hard to reach there but could not make it in time. Then there is another burst of colour along with an excruciating pain in my skull. There is this familiar blur and I see the guy shooting himself, his body falling limp among his child and his wife while the stuffed bunny was soaking up the blood.

I threw up blood on the floor, my body trembling with an unknown foreign feeling. My face, hair, and body were all drowned in sweat with an excruciating pain all over. I saw that my knuckles were covered in blood, my uniform drowned in blood. I felt sticky at my neck. I saw a pair of eyes staring at me while I stared unrecognizably at them. It was quite surprising to see that they held concern in them. I knew I would not last long, so I collapsed on the ground, everything a blur and then something dark covering my vision. I expected to hit the cold floor but instead, I felt a pair of warm hands around my body as I let everything go.

I stirred and opened my eyes. Everything was a huge blur.

Had I lost my eyesight?

Oh I had forgotten that I was 'half blind'.

There were people whispering around me. Or they were talking and I was not able to listen to them properly. Or maybe I was hallucinating. My head ached a bit so I closed my eyes. After a few careful breaths, I opened my eyes. I flinched away from the blinding sunlight which directly attacked my sensitive eyes. I immediately looked towards the interior of the room. There was no one in that room. I was all alone.

My entire body ached, making it difficult for me to move. So I just lay down looking at the closed door while my entire fist was wrapped around in bandages and so was my head, but I was too scared to touch or feel it. I was waiting for someone to walk in and let them know that I was awake.

The entire room was painted white with green curtains on the window. The bar light and the sunlight both bathed the room in light.

There were needles stuck into my arms. One of them leading to the IV stand near my bed while the others to some unknown devices I had no idea about. There were various circular plug-like devices attached on my wrists, chest and back to a machine on my left which seemed to annoy me with its constant beeping.

Observing clearly, I remembered that it was called an electrocardiogram which I had read about in my most hated biology class. There was a fan rotating above my head, a feeling which made me anxious and nervous. No matter how safe it would look, it always scared me, the thought of it falling on me. There was a metal chair near me. The idea of coming into senses with someone waiting for you to wake up was beautiful but sadly there was no one. But then, it didn't matter a bit to me.

I was looking at the plain walls when I heard the door open. I looked at the door to find Artyom entering. It had been a while since I saw him. To be honest, I felt good seeing him. But what freaked me out was to see him in a doctor's coat and glasses. He came near me and sat on the chair.

"You're…"

My throat was parched and hurt. It was as if I had a bad cold or a sore throat.

I panicked.

Did I lose my voice?

"Calm down," he chuckled in his usual jolly humor, handing me a glass of water.

I chugged it all down.

"Just speak slowly," he said.

"You're getting ready for Halloween or what?" I said a bit softly this time, feeling much better.

"No, why would you ask that?" He said laughing a bit.

I pointed at this coat and stethoscope.

"I'm the doctor in the medical wing of the facility," he said still laughing.

I wondered what he found so funny, or maybe that was his jolly self.

"What is this place?" I asked in my hoarse voice.

"The medical wing in the western side," he said focusing on the examination pad in his hands. He was occasionally looking at the devices and back to the pad noting down something.

"You're lucky you survived," he said in a grave voice sighing.

As much as I loathed asking that, my curious self asked anyways.

"Who failed?" I asked quietly.

"I'm afraid I'm not the right person to tell you that," he paused looking thoughtful. "Nor is this the right time," he finished. "Anyone you would like to meet?" He asked.

"Alyosha," the name slipped out of my tongue without realization. Not that I regretted it a bit. She was the only person I could trust and talk to.

Artyom smiled and walked out.

I kept laying there waiting for her to come through if they allowed her.

I had barely closed my eyes when I heard the door creak open. I heard footsteps running towards me.

"Hey!" She said crying and laughing at the same time.

I smiled. I wanted to sit up but my body did not allow it.

"HIII," I greeted her trying to sound as enthusiastic as possible.

She wiped her tears with her sleeves.

"Hey, don't cry..." I said.

"I'm so glad you survived the first test," she said joyously.

"Why don't you sit down?" I said eyeing to the chair and back to her smiling. "And thank you..." I said looking at her.

She reached out to hold my hands but withdrew. Maybe she was scared that she would get infected or maybe she was scared that it would hurt me. I offered her my hand.

"Wouldn't it hurt?" She said hesitating.

"No, it would not," I said laughing softly.

She held onto my hand, her warmth making me feel happy as she stroked my hand.

"My sister passed away like this," she said looking into the void.

"You had a sister?"

"An identical twin sister, yes."

She was smiling thinking about something.

"She was a test subject too," she said looking at my hand with an expressionless face.

"Oh...I'm sorry..." I said keeping quiet after that. I did not know what to say next.

"It's alright. At least she is in a better place," she said smiling.

Death was indeed strange. Now I was unsure if to feel bad or good about it.

"Yeah..." I said.

"Artyom said you will be discharged by tomorrow afternoon," she said.

"Artyom though, he seems strange," I asked.

"I would not say strange but he is so much better than his brother," she said.

"Who is his brother?" I asked.

"Master, of course. Don't you know?" She asked looking surprised.

"Oh lord, really?" I asked, my eyes and mouth all wide in shock.

They don't really look alike though...

She chuckled, "Yes…"

"Did something happen to Fyodor though?" I asked.

"Why would anything happen to him?"

"Why does he hurt people like this? Live human beings..."

"He says that only humans can give him the results of the tests he conducts. In the beginning, he did not know where to bring humans from so he conducted some kind of experiment on himself. I had heard that something had happened to him. He and Artyom were not seen for months until they reappeared again." She said.

That explained the reality he had underneath all that fake makeup.

Of course, he needed humans. No mouse or squirrel would do for the tests he was conducting.

"Do you know why Dasha works here? I mean, what happened to her?" I asked wondering if she knew anything about it.

"The only thing I know is she lost her family. She owed a huge amount of money to master and when asked for it, she and her family planned running away to India where her husband was from. So they were killed and now she has to work here to pay off her debts."

"What happened with the money though?" I asked.

"That's the mystery, she would not tell," she said looking at me.

"And from where do you get such information from?" I asked chuckling.

"Diana knows everything. She is actually master's oldest aunt from her paternal side," she said giggling.

My jaws dropped open.

"What? And you complain about him in front of her? You'll get fired or killed!" I gasped.

"She understands and doesn't mind," she said laughing.

"But still..." I hesitated, continuing with my warnings.

"It's fine," she said still laughing.

"Why is he like this though?" I asked mumbling.

She kept silent for a moment looking very serious.

"He had always been like this since he inherited his father's property. No one knows exactly why. We don't even know who his mother is. This family is packed with mystery," she replied. "Anyway, how are you feeling?" She asked smiling.

"I'm fine, I think," I said smiling a bit.

"Diana is making lunch for you," she said.

"You could have seriously brought anything to eat you know, you did not have to make that old lady work," I said frowning.

"Don't worry, she insisted herself," she said laughing.

"What is she making?" I asked eagerly.

"Chicken pot pie with truffle! God, she makes it sooo gooooodd!!!" She squealed throwing her hands in the air like a kid.

I laughed feeling a lot better by then.

"Well, I'll be waiting for it," I laughed.

She giggled.

"Sure," she said.

We sat there in an awkward silence. I had questions but could not think of any at the moment.

She was holding my hands, the warmth of it hugging my entire body like a mother to her baby. I was drifting off to sleep when I heard a cough.

I tilted my head looking to my side to see Fyodor standing with Artyom behind him.

Alyosha looked down sadly. She let go of my hand and got up scurrying out of the room, looking down as if bowing at them the entire time.

He walked close to my bed, Artyom trailing behind him.

I loathed his presence. What he did the night before was unforgivable. But I was there for all that, right? At least I had a job and a friend unlike others in captivity. I did not know, if to be thankful or angry.

"How are you?" He asked.

"None of your concern," I replied not looking at him.

Artyom giggled.

My eyes were shooting daggers at him. Fyodor gave him a serious look which made him stop laughing.

I looked at the ceiling not wanting to face him.

"What all did you see?" He asked.

"Are you fuckin serious? I literally woke up a few hours ago and you want answers from me? How selfish and insensitive can you be?" I screamed pushing him away.

I saw his jaws tighten. I took a close look at him. His eyes were bloodshot, his hair in a mess. He had not even changed his dress. I knew it was my blood and the others' included.

I screamed curses at him.

"Who did you kill this time?" I yelled again.

"The youngest one," he said walking out while Artyom kept standing there.

I looked away in disgust.

How could he?

Yi Ling? That kid?

I remember being thirteen spending my time watching cartoons and reading comics and now this kid was dead.

"You hurt him," Artyom said.

I held the vas beside my head and threw it at him. He ducked which made me even madder.

He had killed someone; nothing could be more hurtful than that.

"Just go away!" I screamed.

I plopped back to my original place.

I couldn't help but break down hard. I missed Daniel. I wondered what had happened back at home.

Has Daniel moved on to finding someone new?

My thoughts traveled back to those times when we used to text continuously for hours together.

"What if I vanish one day from here?" I had once questioned him.

"I would search for you in each and every corner of the universe and find you out. I won't rest till I made you mine."

That was what he had said.

I wondered if those were just his words or if he really meant it.

As crazy and desperate my inner demands were, I was mentally screaming.

Where are you, Daniel?

What about your promises?

I was too tired to think of anything. For the moment, crying seemed the best option. So that was what I did.

Again...

Treatment

I woke up to the ceiling fan rotating above my head, the impact of the artificial illumination of the bar light in the room overpowering my senses.

The windows were cold, it was already dark outside.

My stomach growled. I looked down at my poor hungry stomach. Maybe they had decided not to approach me due to what happened in the afternoon. I heard voices outside the room, one of which I could recognize was of Artyom. I heard shuffling of feet which stopped after several minutes. I could see a pair of pointed leather shoes stopping at the door, but I could not really make out whose that was until it opened to reveal the younger brother of the two.

"Ah! You're awake!" He exclaimed happily.

"What do you want?" I said grumpily.

I noticed that the shards of the porcelain glass vase had been cleaned up.

"Just wanted to talk to you. I hope you don't mind me coming in," he said.

"Funny of you to say that," I replied sarcastically. "All you people have ever done is to invade random people's privacy and destroying their lives and now you're asking for my permission for a mere thing as this, and that too in your own property."

I saw a tablet in his coat pocket.

"Never mind," he said walking in.

"What do you want anyway? Why are you here?" I asked him

in a deadly voice.
"Um...I'm here for my brother."
"That monster?"
"He is not a monster and he has a name."
"Whatever,"
"I think he has taken a liking to you."
I kept quiet for a moment after his statement which I found way too delirious.
"He is not capable of any positive emotion. Besides I'm here for something else."
"I have never seen him this sane before."
"Not my place to interfere in his life and or any of his personal issues."
"Please, just please help him."
I glared at him.
"It's me who needs help!" I barked. "Besides I like someone else."
It was a true fact though.
"That guy you're talking about has moved on."
I laughed.
"You don't even know who that is!" I exclaimed flailing my arms.
"Daniel Ross. We know everything."
I was tongue-tied for a few minutes.
"How do you know...?" I asked trailing off.
"Doesn't matter,"
I closed my eyes.
"It does," I said taking in a deep breath and letting it all out. I was trying my best not to cry. Even the slightest possibility of that happening had scared me so much.
"What proof do you have?" I asked sighing, reopening my eyes.
"Facebook," he said," Instagram and kik."
I remembered him asking me to open a facebook account but I could not since I was too scared that my parents would find

out.

He opened his facebook account and gave me the tablet.

I felt extremely happy seeing his photograph.

“Hey! That’s him,” I said smiling, gliding my fingers across the screen which slid down to show his posts.

Tears started gliding down my cheeks when I saw his posts. There were pictures of him with some brunette. There was also a picture of him smooching her on her lips.

“Do you have discord?” I asked looking at him trying hard to swallow tears.

“I don’t but I can get it if you want,” he said opening playstore and downloading it for me.

Maybe what they say is true. Maybe online relationships are just for fun. People don’t take it seriously. I remember a friend laughing at me when I had told her that I was in an online relationship. She had told me that it would never work out and here I was sitting on a bed, all bandaged up and facing my worst nightmares.

“There you go,” he said handing me the tablet again.

I logged in my account.

I saw a romantic gif which made me sob even more. I had not been able to reply that night.

I typed a ‘hi’.

There was a long bot message which summed up to say, ‘There is a network connection or you’ve been blocked by the user. Please try again.’

Oh...that’s what he did...

He blocked me.

It felt like a knife went straight through my heart.

All the dreams and hopes I had went right to the trash.

All the confidence I had into flames.

Artyom rubbed my arm.

“It’s alright, it happens.”

“Ever loved someone from your heart and soul and then find

out that they don't give a shit?" I asked.

"I haven't but Fyodor has," he replied quietly.

"It is painful when the only person you rely on drifts away," I said clutching onto the pillow, my body racking hard with sobs.

"Believe it or not, for a moment I felt like I was talking to Fyodor. His talks are often thoughtful. Sometimes too deep that my head hurts so much from thinking," he said laughing.

"I heard you and Fyodor are brothers,"

"Brothers from different mothers."

"And how's that?"

"Our father was a male nympho, basically. He slept with a stripper and got Fyodor while I tagged a year later by another. Our father was actually kind enough to take us both in and get us educated."

"That's actually kind of him."

"It is,"

"What happened to Fyodor though?"

"You mean how he started killing people and being a deranged criminal?"

I meant to know the entire thing but anyway.

"Yes."

"He was a quiet kid. Doing everything by himself. He lived in isolation. No matter how friendly we tried being, he dwelt in his own little world. He fell for a girl when he was sixteen though. Her father called him a bastard which blew him up. And what maddened him next was that the girl said something bad to him and dumped him. So he decided to stay at home. But what happened next was utterly unexpected."

"What happened?"

"He just started reading and reading. He read dad's all business books, all comics and then he went for grandpa's old medicine books."

I was lapping up his story like a puppy.

"Then what?"

"He would spend hours reading science books in the library.

Dad even got grandpa's lab opened so that he could perform his own experiments."

"Woah...you people have your personal laboratory here?"

"It belonged to our grandpa, yes. We even had our own stock of chemicals and a dealer to get them here. We bribed him so that he won't tell the cops that we own such stuff without a license,"

"But what if you're caught?"

"There's very less chance. Besides dad has left behind huge acres of land on which we farm and earn a lot of money. And he pays everyone generously so no one would ever betray. Besides he deals in health potions with certain gangs who are our allies and helps destroy people who go against us."

"Dasha..."

"Yes, Dasha's family was killed that way."

"How could he kill a child?" I asked tears welling up in my eyes.

"We wanted to confront them actually. The entire murder thing was an accident. Besides Dasha was involved in some drug dealing business so she took money from us. We never leak the original stuff to people to avoid getting caught."

"What are health potions?"

"The reason you can go without food for days."

That was how I was surviving without food for days together.

"How does it work?"

"I hardly know much about it. But I do know that it multiplies the Adenosine triphosphate molecules in the body to replenish it with energy even if we are sleeping or doing anything. It's like food in a small dosage."

"How do you gather information about your test subjects?"

"Fyodor has his sources. Besides the employees that we send to get them, are high-class internet hackers and doctors."

That explained how Daniil used to professionally inject me with needles and stuff even at the harshest moments.

"It's funny how your hackers don't know how to play games," I said rolling my eyes.

Artyom chuckled.

"Boris is the best hacker we have got," he said smiling.

"Sure," I said shrinking back to my mattress.

"Why was I kept in a brothel?" I asked, my eyes blurry with tears thinking about Mauni. The flashback of the man I killed was making my heart beat faster and making me anxious, and above that all, filling me with an unknown sense of sorrow, regret, and fear.

"That was your first test. The rest of the kids picked were put to death. I remember Fyodor being very excited that night when he received that call."

I made a face.

"And why would he be that hyper to know that someone killed someone else?"

"That's because we have never had any test subject of that mentality. The kids with the highest tolerance are usually picked. We have never had any subject killing anyone before. We choose subjects of plain and sensitive mentality. That's what he likes about you, that you are full of surprises. No one would dare to fight him, but you did. Even if you knew that could kill you, you never backed off. You never gave up. That is what he keeps looking for, someone who would not give up on him."

"Basically he wants someone to run after him," I scoffed mockingly.

"He wants someone to run after, a person who would not judge him by the way he looks, a person with who he can be the way he originally was. He wants to relive...to start over. But the things that he has done before can never make the situation normal, ever. He just wants things to be easier to embrace. It's strange that he wants to change when he never wanted to. I've never seen him this needy before..." He said trailing off.

I kept sitting there quietly. I had no words. This entire drama was too dramatic for me yet then, situations turn the person the way they are and the way their mind works. You really can't do anything about it.

"How did he get that green skin and those bumps on his skin?" I asked trying to search for the correct words to put it in such a way that it didn't sound that offensive.

"He consumed one of his own compounds that he made just because he did not have anyone to test on. We started looking for him when he did not show up during supper. We found him in the lab."

"Maybe mutation," I asked shrugging.

"Wow..." He laughed. "You have got the brains. And yes, it was a mild form of mutation but he pulled through which is good."

I hate science.

"Can't he be cured? Like, get to his original self?"

"He has a formula for an antidote but he is unsure if that will work."

"Why did they kill her?..."

"Kill who?"

"Mauni..."

"The girl back at the brothel you were in? We heard about it all."

"We had to...she could have gotten us caught and we could not really have afforded that."

"You could have talked to her, she had dreams..."

He kept quiet while my sobs filled the entire room.

"It was all my fault...I should never have suggested that," I whispered.

This was a regret I had to live with my entire life.

I had destroyed someone's life.

I had taken something from her that she deserved.

I was a fool.

I was reckless.

How unthoughtful of me...

Artyom rubbed my back.

"Well, at least she is in a better place."

The confusion that had arisen in my mind when I was talking to Alyosha arose again.

Maybe these people used this excuse to drink it all without

feeling guilty, or maybe they did feel guilty and this was a temporary cover up to push away all the bad thoughts that came with it.

But sometimes you have to wait for certain answers, for seeking and getting answers yourself has a greater value and an everlasting effect than just asking and extracting it from others.

"Why does he kill...? Do humans bear no value for him?... All those innocent teens dying just for his experiments. This is unfair." I asked wondering.

"He respects nature but humans. He does not like them even if he is one. He has never had a good experience with them."

"He is not to blame I guess, maybe that was the way he was brought up. I have encountered nice people before," I smiled wiping my tears with the sheets.

"You're lucky then."

"I'm fighting for my life here, which is not being lucky."

"I bet he is being partial this time."

"What do you mean?"

"He is killing all the candidates, saving you. He is even going against his protocol. Killing Rebecca Nissan that way was never in his plans."

"Can't you ask him about his thoughts and what his intentions are?"

"He barely talks to anyone but Uncle Gaines during meals."

"Wait, the old man who sits on his right?"

He chuckled.

"Quite an observer, aren't you?"

"It was not that difficult to spot really," I said warding off his flattery praises.

"Now you're being too modest."

"I'm not,"

Artyom was about to say something next when we heard the door knock.

He turned back still sitting on the chair.

“Come in!” He said raising his voice.

I saw Alyosha walk in with a moving table.

She opened the door and walked in, stopping for a moment when she saw Artyom, her cheeks getting a coating of pink on them.

“M...master Valentine?” She said stuttering.

“Valentine? I thought your name was Artyom,” I asked confused fighting the urge to laugh at how funny that sounded.

“Oh, that is my middle name. Only a few people here know my first name,”

he said still looking at the blushing Alyosha.

He was still looking at her grinning.

There had to be something going on between them.

How had Alyosha never mentioned that to me before?

“Dooooo...you two have a thing going on?” I said feeling sick.

Somehow this reminded me of those cheezy romantic couples back at school.

I looked away since I never found such things appealing.

She scurried to me and placed the tray near me and I was forced to look that way wondering what was in there. That was when I saw Artyom pulling her into his lap.

She got up in an instant.

“M...master...” She said with her voice extremely low.

I made a gagging face.

“Get a room, jeez,” I said looking away.

He chuckled petting her on her head.

“I should let you two bond alone,” he said getting up and going out of the room.

She sighed in relief, still as red as a tomato.

“What’s going on between you two?” I said almost jumping at her.

“Calm down,” she said laughing.

I pouted like a kid.

“Aww,” she said giggling. “We are dating,” she revealed.

"Whaaaat?" I exclaimed squishing my face with my own hands. I was beyond surprised. "How did it all happen?" I asked laughing.

"A year ago. He was helping me in the orchards picking apples and we kept talking like, for one whole day and he ended up asking me out, I think, after a month and a half maybe?"

"Young love," I said laughing softly.

She huffed and crossed her arms sneering at me which made me laugh.

She laughed and let go of her arms back to normal.

"Look what I got for you," she said pulling the tray to her lap.

I eyed the plate greedily.

There was a shorter but wider version of a coffee mug, with its top covered with a doughy bread-like substance.

"Ooh that looks yummy," I said rubbing my hands which made her chuckle.

She tore the bread open revealing a thick soup in the mug. I could see pieces of chicken, peas, and carrots swimming in the gravy. I could see steam from the gravy which was clearly visible against her black apron.

She dipped the bread in the gravy and brought it near my lips.

I chewed on the food for a while.

"This is so good!" I exclaimed my eyes wide open.

That was the best food I had in ages.

She laughed feeding me again.

I tried hard to swallow back tears.

She reminded me of one of my aunts and how she used to feed me as a kid when I was sick.

I knew one thing. I could not get attached to anyone for the people I had grown closer and closer to, had hurt me worse and worse. My head was aching hard and letting go of all the thoughts for a moment seemed like a better idea.

She kept feeding me and put away the dish when it was over. I'd admit that I was full. She gave me water to drink.

"Um…actually Master made this…" She said.

"Who? Artyom?" I asked.

"No."

"Please don't tell me he made it," I gave her an upset look.

"He is melting," she said laughing hard. "God, I've never seen him like this before."

I scrunched my eyebrows.

"Can we just not talk about him?" I asked.

She cleared her throat and gave me a glass of water to drink. I was about to drink that when she asked me to wait.

"Hey, hold on for a second."

I looked at her.

"What?" I asked her.

She pulled out a small bottle of pills.

"What are these?" I asked her looking at the pills.

"Medicines," she said handing me two of different types.

I popped them in my mouth and gulped the water.

"I hope you're not drugging me," I said giggling.

She laughed.

"Not really. Master said you are completely stable, beside you were on dialysis. Your system is empty from the test drug. These are just painkillers," she smiled.

"How do you know that?" I asked grinning.

"I study in the evenings with Valentine. He teaches me stuff," she said blushing.

"Awwww," I teased her.

"Stop!" She whisper-yelled pulling the sheets to my neck.

"Wait, how long was I out for?" I asked her the question popped out of my mind from nowhere.

"Four days," she said frowning a bit. "I was scared."

I could not believe I was out for that long.

"What about the others?" I asked.

"The other two guys are being treated down in the basement by Dasha while the youngest girl...well..." she stopped her lashes drooping down.

"You don't have to talk about it…" I said and then keeping quiet hence. "You should go and rest."

She sighed getting up and stroked my head for the last time before she went.

"Thank you…" I said looking at her and smiling slightly.

"No problem. A friend in need is a friend indeed," she said smiling. I saw her switching off the light and switching on the night bulb which glowed softly before leaving me.

"Sleep well, I'll visit you in the morning," she said, her face barely visible when I heard the door close.

I stared at the rotating fan above my head and drifted off.

I woke up in the middle of the night when I felt that someone was putting a duct tape on my mouth. My eyes shot wide open to reveal that a person had indeed taped my mouth. I pushed him away but he caught me, blocking my arms in his firm grip. My heart was beating hard. I was almost in tears. Who are they? What did they want? I shook violently trying to get rid of him. I managed to hit his nose with my forehead.

"Shit! This bitch!" He said squishing me closer to his body to stop me from moving.

I recognized that voice.

Wait, Fyodor?

I observed him properly looking up. I could see a pair of braces shining in the moonlight that came from the window. Technically, the light from the bulb was not enough to show anything clearly.

But why was he taping my mouth?

What is he doing?

He had my entire body trapped within his arms which made me immobile.

His body was cold and smelled fresh. Maybe he had taken a shower. He smelled of lime and musk which drove me dizzy. The full sleeves of his furry night robe rubbing against my bare arms gave me chills in the spine. There were goosebumps on my arms. I felt dirty and stale as compared to him. I was still groaning while my mouth was taped shut. The tape made me feel nauseous and uncomfortable. He gripped my shoulders tight and made me lay on the bed.

He put his index finger on his plump lips.

"Shhh," he shushed me down.

I calmed down and looked at him with curious eyes. The ruby red stone on his finger ring was sparkling in the moonlight. He pulled out a dropper bottle from his robe pocket. He placed it on the table where Alyosha had previously kept her tray on. He carefully unwrapped the bandage of my head, my entire self twitching from the pain. My head had not healed yet. He kneeled by my bedside and slid his arm under my head, his arm serving as a pillow to me while his other arm clutching on to my arm to draw me closer to him. He extended his arm and pulled out the dropper which had some kind of liquid.

I desperately hoped it was not some sick joke of his.

He pulled me closer, my nose buried into his chest. I was shivering uncontrollably almost in tears. He squeezed out the entire content on the injured parts of my head and I felt as if I was about to die. There was an excruciating pain on my head. I knew he was doing something bad to me. I was thrashing my hands and legs. I was pushing him hard trying to pull away from him. Screw sexist Mother Nature and her making the male race stronger. He kept pulling me against him. He was rubbing my back hard and fast.

What the hell is he doing?

What is this!

Why is it hurting that bad?

I wanted to scream out loud. If not for the tape on my mouth, I would have woken up the entire household with my screams. The pain and the burning sensation were cutting through my skin like a scissor through the paper. He was cradling and rocking my body and rubbing my back as if to comfort me. I felt as if he was trying to give me a comforting death. Or it was one of his experiments on me which were failing painfully and miserably. I knew my senses were fading away from me. I could not bear it. I opened my closed eyes, my face squished within his furry robe when I felt everything fading to a far distance and that was when I felt a pair of soft, warm lips on my forehead which shocked me but it was too late. I was not in a condition to stay awake, or in my senses anymore to have let go.

My eyes fluttered open to the bright afternoon sun. I turned to a side to see several pairs of worried eyes looking at me to which I was taken aback.

“Woah!” I said. “What’s wrong with you people?”

I felt a bit free and loose.

I remembered what had happened the previous night.

I saw my hands. They had no bandages on them. They were completely healed as if nothing had happened to them in the first place. My eyes went wide as realization dawned on me. I put my hands on my head. I was shocked to see that it had healed completely. There was no pain.

There were Artyom and Alyosha. Even Diana was there, her arm locked with the older gentleman whom I had seen at the breakfast table the other day. *Uncle Gaines, aah!*

“Why are you staring at me like that?” I asked them giving a weird look.

“I don’t understand...” Artyom said looking confused.

“How did you heal that fast?” , Alyosha asked with a confused expression.

I saw Fyodor walk into the room.

He looked at them right in the eye causing them to walk out of the room.

‘Hey, don’t leave me alone, ’ I mentally yelled.

If only telepathic communication were real.

He had something in his hand which he handed to me. It was a mirror with a brass frame.

I sat up sitting on the pillow. He shook his head and patted my back causing me to move forward. He picked up the pillow and placed it against the headboard making a backrest for me.

"Sit," he said in his usual deep voice while I leaned back on the pillow embarrassed.

I looked in the mirror. The places where I had injuries were clear, just like my hands while the places where I had hair; the hair seemed longer than the usual length I had. I looked funny but was cured completely.

I wanted to thank him. But I was supposed to be mad at him, right?

"How are you feeling?" He asked.

I looked at him. His eyebrows almost touching each other. He seemed as if he was annoyed.

"Good," I said and looked away from him.

Maybe he had nothing to say. The thought of the way he had me captured me in his arms the night before filled me with an unknown feeling.

We sat there in an awkward silence for about ten minutes, maybe.

He had his hands on his knees while I stared at the empty wall far in front of me.

He got up and started walking out.

"Hey..." I interrupted him abruptly, scared myself if I did something wrong.

He stopped and twisted his head sideways to me.

"Thank you..." I could not help but blurt it out.

His back was at me but I could see him looking at his shoes, his hands now inside his pant pockets on either side, partially covered by the flaps of his coat.

"Ne problema," he mumbled and walked out hurriedly.

I kept wondering what he said. Did it mean 'no problem'?

Ne for no and problema for problem. Sounded almost like it.

I was still in my thought process when Artyom came in running looking eager about something, followed by Alyosha.

"What happened?" He asked wiggling his eyebrows.

"Nothing..." I said looking at them raising one of my eyebrows.

“How did you get well so fast?” Artyom asked making a Sherlock’s face.

“He came in at late night and used his antidote on me,” I said unsure how to act.

I saw someone had cleaned my body and put on clean clothes on me.

“IT HAS TO BE THE ANTIDOTE!” he gasped and squealed.

“Calm down your tits” I said rolling my eyes.

He started pacing around the room anxiously.

“What happened now? Why are you being like this?” I asked him irritated.

“He is turning into...a normal person,” Alyosha said.

“Exactly,” he reacted.

“Well, that’s a good thing, right?” I asked.

“Of course!” He exclaimed.

Bonding

"I should probably get working," I said straining myself off the bed.

"Oh no, no, no," Artyom said lifting my legs to the bed again.

"But I'm bored," I said whining.

"Or do you want to see him?" Artyom said with an evil smile lingering on his face.

"No," I said rolling my eyes. "I'm tired of staying at the bed and doing nothing." I said huffing.

"Let me check your vitals and see when you can be discharged," Artyom said walking out of the room while Alyosha remained beside me.

"There's so less tension in here since you came," Alyosha said. "Diana is grateful to you."

"Stop making me feel..." I was at loss of words." Like a God or something. It's him who is being like this. And it's not certain that I'll live. I may fail the test and get killed too," I said bluntly.

"I know, but it's amazing the way he is drawn to you," she said quietly.

"I myself don't know why," I said looking down. "But I don't hope for miracles because life isn't a fairytale," I said looking at my dirty nails.

We heard footsteps and in walked Artyom.

He pulled out a syringe.

"Oh god, not this," I said rubbing my forehead.

"Just a small blood test," he said.

He tied the velcro strip around my arm as tight as possible which enabled the blood to flow down.

He felt my skin with his thumb probably trying to search for my blood vessels. He prepped the injection and I saw the needle vanish into my skin. Strangely, it didn't hurt anymore. He took the syringe out of the room, vanishing to the left.

"I need to shower," I said. "I feel like a dirty pig."

That made Alyosha laugh.

"You want hot water to bathe?" She asked.

"Of course not! It's so hot" I said looking out of the window.

It was unusually sunny that day.

Artyom walked in again.

"So, when can I be discharged?" I asked.

"Well, you can move around and take a walk if you want," he said looking very busy with his notes in his arms.

I shook my head and walked out of the room.

I knew I had access to the basement down, through my own fingerprints. I strutted down the hallway through the stairs and kept roaming in the empty corridors when I realized that I had lost my way among the maze of rooms, when I had not asked for it in the first place. I was kind of hoping for running into someone. After a few turns, I saw an opened room. I could hear the tip tap noise as if someone was typing on a laptop or a computer keyboard.

Who would have their office in such a weird, isolated place?

Wondering hard, I peeked into the room to find Fyodor typing away like a machine on his laptop. I was too scared to approach him but then there was no one around. So I decided to slip across the room without being spotted and find someone else for helping me.

I kept peeking into his room waiting for a moment when he would be dead focused on his work so that I could tiptoe and slip through, and that was when I heard him saying, "Are you done peeking into my office?"

My face went red with embarrassment.

When did he see me?

I came out from my hiding place.

"Um…I lost my way." I said.

"Lost your way? You don't even know the way," he said looking up at me from his laptop.

God, why did they not stop me?

I was angry at Alyosha and Artyom. That could be the reason they were giggling when I wandered off away from the room.

"I'll just go find someone to lead me to the basement," I said and walked out.

"Wait!" I heard him say raising his voice but not particularly yelling.

I did not want to stop but something stopped me.

"Yes?" I stepped back and looked into the room watching him stand up and closing his laptop.

"I'll escort you to the basement. I don't want you to be a walking disaster all around here."

I frowned.

"I make food and clean your house like a fucking maid so there's no way I'll turn this place into a walking disaster."

He unbuttoned his coat button which made me look down even though there was no reason to look away as he was not getting nude or anything. I saw him getting ahead of me.

"Are you coming or not?" He said in his usual grumpy manner.

I said nothing but just started walking behind him when he resumed his walk to show me the way. A part of me was embarrassed to what had happened the night before. It was weird the way I felt every time he was around me. My heartbeat would go up suddenly, my face would go red and hot and out of nowhere I would start feeling jittery and hyperactive. It was a pain to hide it all. I'll admit I felt jealous when he was acting like that with Rebecca and the fact Artyom said that he liked me made things more awkward for me to be around him.

My limbs ached really badly. I leaned against the wall panting like a dog and groaning. He stopped walking and looked behind at me. He gave me a glance as if he was concerned. Or maybe, it was just me assuming things. I was an expert at this. I was a desperate girl; desperate for love, attention and care. All those things beyond my reach were what I was so eager for. And, something I lacked was self respect. People would slap and kick me and yet I would help them.

The fact that he liked me was bullshit. I needed someone who would treat me like a queen, not like a maid, someone who would actually fill my dry life with greenery and Fyodor was not like that. There was a bit of hope left in me, and I did not want to waste that on someone like him. There were plenty of chances he could ruin me completely. Now was not the time to fall in love and miracles. I had always hoped for one which never happened and I could not trust it would ever happen especially in such a dangerous condition. This was one selfish man who never hesitated to kill other people, even kids. What made me so special that he could fall for me? I trusted no one, not even him.

My parents used to hit me and after a while they would pamper me for the moment just to hurt me again. I had a belief he was doing the same. He hurt me at first, healed me just to hurt me again. I had met a lot of people who could put out a fake smile and extract whatever they wanted out of you and it was unimaginable they way they could turn to the exact opposite the moment all their work was over.

I felt someone lift me up. I looked up to see his brown eyes which were already glaring down at me. He started walking briskly. This could not continue anymore. This was it, now or never.

"Stop." I said letting out a sigh.

He did not stop.

"I said, STOP! PLEASE!" I yelled loudly punching hard at his chest.

He stopped and looked down at me. I could see a tinge of hurt on his face. It did not take more than a few seconds for it to get replaced by anger. He pushed me down to the floor from his arms with a disgusted look and walked off.

I watched him walk off till he vanished round the corner. I could not help but cry. I felt it in my heart this time. I could feel a tear slide down my cheek, and another till I could not contain it any longer. I sat there huddling myself, crying as much as I wanted to. I stared at the blank walls and the closed doors for a while before falling into an unconscious state of siesta.

I woke up, not having my eyes opened yet. I was sleeping on something really soft. My leg was on somebody's waist while my small fingers were gripping onto a garment. I took a whiff and smelled cologne.

My eyes shot open when I saw that I was in a kind of...cuddling posture. I heard small snores and looked up at the source to find Fyodor sleeping peacefully.

What am I doing on his bed?

My thoughts travelled back to the time when I had fallen asleep on the corridor.

What a stupid thing to do.

He had his arms around me in a tight grip. Not tight enough to kill me though. It was almost as if, he was in a protective stance. It felt like he would not let anyone take me away.

My body was aching with sleeping in that position for so long.

Surprisingly, I felt calm. Never had I ever expected myself to feel calm sleeping next to such a brutal person.

Even if I wanted to be there, I felt the need to go away.

I could not risk getting close to him and being told later that I was not enough.

That I was not compatible.

That I was not enough.

That I was not meant to be.

Even if they said he might have feelings for me.

I tried to pry his arms away, in trial to escape.

I was just about to hold his hands to remove them, my hands trembling hard, that was when he grabbed my arms and pulled me to him.

His eyes were wide, his face still emotionless while I gazed back into his.

He had not yet removed his makeup but he had indeed removed his contacts.

An unknown sense of relief washed over me.

He had his arm wrapped around me; my body on his arms while he held close to me, extremely close, while he held onto my wrist of the same hand with which I had tried to remove his.

"Where do you think you were going?" He asked in a husky sleepy voice causing my heart rate to pick up it's crazy fast pace, a cluster of butterflies fluttering all over my stomach.

"Basement," I squeaked.

"This is your home from now on," he said in a whispering voice.

"N...no..." I managed to stutter out.

I shifted a little feeling uncomfortable with the same posture. He noticed my discomfort.

He lifted me and put me on him. I was lying on his body looking down at him.

"What are you doing?" I asked him in a low voice.

He rolled his eyes and turned me to the other side, still holding me close.

"Just holding you close," he said.

My face went hot and red.

"Treat me as a slave you brought me here as," I said.

"It's unfair to treat a queen as a maid, besides you have done enough," he said in a 'matter of fact' tone.

There was an internal chaos going on in my body.

"I'm no queen," I said rolling my eyes.

"A queen never knows if she is. It's the job of her subjects to decide if she is the real deal or not."

"Then I'm afraid you have poor judging standards."

"I don't care."

I sighed.

"Why are we even having this conversation?" I asked.

I saw his face lose all of its confidence, his face contorting into that of regret and pain while tears starting rolling down his cheeks like an endless waterfall.

I could do nothing but watch.

A part of me was shocked.

"Why are you crying?" I asked him unmoved.

"I want to change, please help me," he pleaded holding both of my hands.

"You seriously think I'll fall for this?" I asked.

I had never seen him like this. He indeed looked disturbed, traumatized, tensed and stressed.

"It's easy, surrender to the police yourself."

"It's foolish and I don't want to die," he said breaking into another fit of tears.

"Now you realize how serious death is. You just go on killing people like you swat flies, playing with lives is not a game."

He hugged me close and started sobbing into my shoulder.

"It's too late for a change, isn't it?" He asked, his tears making my shoulders wet as I lay there taken aback, transfixed and staring at nowhere but lost in my thoughts.

He looked like a man in regret, craving for a change.

But he had sinned...a lot...

I wanted to caress his back and coo into his ears that everything would be alright but I could not give him false hopes.

Did this monster deserve mercy? A bit of sympathy? That too from the victim?

"It's never too late for a change."

I was surprised at myself when those words came tumbling out of my mouth.

He looked up at me, while I shifted my gaze down at him.

I looked into his beautiful orbs.

Shame

Anger
Frustration
Regret
And yet a will...
A will to change...

"Why do you want to change though?" I asked. "You seem to be happy with this life."

"Anger...it made me do ridiculous things. But now when it has all been vented out, I realize..." He said looking at me.

"Look, I need a chance to change, someone to live for, life seems so pointless...I want to shed off my bad past..." He said trailing off.

"But it will cost you a lot," I mumbled.

A lot, I'll say...

Lives are priceless; money can't pay for what you have done...

Or the injustice...

"I don't want to get into trouble. Can you think of any other way of repentance?" He asked blinking.

As far as I knew, there was no other way of repentance.

"I don't want to hide anymore, this is killing me..." He said.

"You want people to accept you...You want people to appreciate you...You don't want to be hated or scared of...You don't want to live with secrets..." I whispered.

"Yes..." He mumbled back." I want to leave this life and start over, a better life...where I can be a better version of myself..." He said squeezing my hands a little more. "Please, help me..."

I looked down at the empty space between us.

"You want to let all of this go?"

"Yes,"

"You want to get things back to right?"

"Yes,"

"Are you willing to give what it takes?"

He kept silent.

I knew he was scared.

"I'm scared," he said, again...

I looked at him. My continuous gaze forcing him to look my way.

"Fear is not an answer,"

"What if they give me a death sentence?" He asked. "I wouldn't be able to start anew. I know with what I have done...there is no way they will have any mercy on me..."

I knew it was a difficult question to answer.

If only he had thought of it earlier.

But the past was gone, everything already done. No one could change it.

All you could change is what is to come.

The future...

"That would be even better," I said.

He looked at me for a really long time.

"Oh,"

"This is what you think of me," he said.

I smiled at him, a small sad one.

"Looking at the positive side of life," I said.

Tears were welling up in my eyes.

I could not realize when I fell for him so deep and hard.

And it was my choice.

"It's not goddamn positive!" He said in an angry voice.

I hugged him tightly.

He froze for a moment, his breath turning normal.

"The universe will give you another chance," I said in a muffled voice.

I could feel his arms wrapping around me.

"What do you mean?"

"Even if you die, you'll be reborn, given another chance to live your life as a whole different person. The universe always forgives her children despite their sins. You will live a new life,"

He kept quiet for a moment.

"But you never know..." was all he said.
"All you can do is to have faith and belief…" I whispered back.
"Do you believe in God?" He asked looking thoughtful.
"The universe is my God and her rules are my laws to obey and abide by. Everyone has their own views I guess. This is a really controversial topic. It depends on who you believe in and who you respect, but in the end, you have to stick together with people around you and leave in peace." I said looking up at the ceiling.
He let out an uneasy sigh and laid down closing his eyes while I looked at him.
"That's deep..." He said softly.
"It's my philosophy...of life...Yours might be different. Everyone has their own philosophy."
It was incredulous of how calm I felt. There was no tension in the air. I felt calm and peaceful. It was as if things were changing.
"Your repentance comes with a heavy price....." I stated.
"I know..."
"The only way you can cleanse yourself is-"
"Holy water,"
I looked at him giving him a strange look.
"No," I said laughing a bit.
He chuckled as well.
"Then what?" He asked in a serious voice drawing closer to me.
"Forgive all those who have done wrong to you and repent for your mistakes, with a true heart..." I said looking intently into his eyes.
He was not really a bad person.
His anger and frustration had caused all of this to happen.
After all, who hates power?
This is a power hungry world, after all...
Everyone wants to have control on other people to make themselves feel superior.

They don't know how stupid they look when they act this away.

Desperate.

Desperate for power.

Desperate for authority.

They indeed made me laugh.

Why not accept life the way it is and try to improve things than starting to act ridiculous.

He yawned making me yawn as well.

I had a strange tendency to yawn when I saw others yawn as well. At times I wondered if that was normal or was it just me.

"Are you sleepy? Or, hungry too maybe?" He asked concerned.

"I just want to sleep. Why? Are you hungry?" I asked.

"No, I want to sleep as well. These years have tired me out," he said.

I smiled at him while he smiled down at me.

He hugged me close enveloping my body in his warmth, playing with my hair.

This felt perfect as if it was meant to be...

"I'm sorry I wasn't there for you when you needed me," he whispered.

"So am I."

We are on the same page on this one perhaps.

"Um...can I ask something?" He asked.

"Sure," I said.

"Can I take you out on a date tomorrow?" He paused.

A soft blush crept to my cheeks.

"I've never been on one before," I said.

"Ooh, Am I your first date ever?" He asked laughing softly booping my nose.

"Stop!" I exclaimed laughing.

He squeezed me tight.

"I'll make sure I'm your first and last ever."

As much I wanted to lose myself in the moment and blindly

believe his words, I couldn't...unless he proved them by himself...

"You'll have to earn me," I said in an honest voice.

"I won't stop trying till I get your validation," he said with an earnest voice.

"Where are we going though?" I asked.

"That's a surprise," he said rubbing my back and smiling. "I'll be with you for the entire day tomorrow."

"Is that even a thing? I thought date was like...a dinner or something?" I asked wondering.

"Well, you have all of my attention for the entire day tomorrow," he said still smiling.

There was something in his voice which I hadn't been able to find in anyone else's. He gave me that sense of assurance that I was craving for.

I smiled and snuggled closer into his chest.

I was lost in my crowded thoughts when he said something which cleared my head in an instant before I passed out.

"I love you..."

"I love you too..."

My body felt sore from so much sleeping.

I woke up to no one beside me.

I sat up yawning and stretching, a bit disappointed that Fyodor wasn't there.

I looked around wondering where he could have been when I heard someone turning on the shower in the bathroom.

Must be him.

My face blushed hard at the thought of him in the shower, without clothes, all naked.

I mentally slapped my head.

I had to be a pervert.

I got out of the bed and walked around the room for a bit when I saw the messy bed.

It seemed as if they had removed the old bed, the one in which he had killed Rebecca and replaced it with a new one.

I folded the sheets and placed them carefully on the bed, arranging the pillows next.

"What are you doing?" I heard someone say behind me.

I turned to find Fyodor standing with nothing but a white Turkish towel around his waist.

I saw his bumpy skin and face. It didn't look that bad after all. It seemed as if he had some serious acne issue, but his skin looked kind of bruised and greenish which made me feel awkward.

He had a nice body though, lean muscles and toned abs.

He looked beautiful to me, nonetheless his situation.

I looked down immediately, trying to control my hormones. My heart was beating faster and my entire face getting hotter.

"Arranging the bed."

"We have maids to do that, silly," he said chuckling. It sounded almost as if he was mocking or teasing me.

"Fine," I said still looking down.

"You can look up, you know," he said.

"Um...no thanks," I said, my lips in a thin straight line.

He laughed but walked to me anyway, causing me to walk back as I peeked up at him.

He laughed hard and went past me. He opened the cupboard and pulled out a paper bag and handed it to me.

"This is your dress," he said handing it to me still laughing while I looked at him smiling like an idiot.

I was just about to walk when he pulled me into a hug. I could feel his cold chest against my warm face and sweet fragrance.

I stayed like that all flushed while I held my package.

"Thanks," I mumbled smiling softly as he kissed my head.

"Don't shower yet," he said.

I looked up at him surprised.

"Why?"

"I've called in Deborah to give you a haircut," he said.

I looked at myself in the mirror across the room. My hair indeed looked weird.

"You should go and get dressed," I said.

"Mhm," he said kissing my cheek as I saw him vanish into his walk-in closet.

Rich people and their rich things.

I sat in the bed and peeked into the packet. There was a garment in there. It felt expensive and really soft. I felt the packet from the outside and there were a few metal accessories at the bottom. I was struggling to get my hand inside the packet when I heard someone knock on the door.

I saw Fyodor peeking out from his closet. He hurriedly latched his buttons and yelled.

'Come in!"

I saw an emo girl walk in.

Her hair was in layers and reached down to her ears while her face looked pale and ghostly. Her hair was grey, just like the clouds on a stormy day and so were her eyes, cold and sharp. She had a lip piercing and nose piercing. Her ears, however, caught my attention. She must have had thousands of piercings in her earlobes. Her eyes were clad in black makeup in exact contrast to her skin. She wore a short yet fashionable dress with tons of bracelets and a back choker. The leather boots clicked to the floor as she walked in.

I did not realize I had been watching her with a gaping mouth for that long.

"I know she is quite a show stopper but you need to close your mouth," Fyodor chuckled as he pushed my lower jaw up, closing my mouth.

I blushed a little looking at the stylist, flashing a smile at her.

She did not smile though, but maintained her straight face while I looked at Fyodor.

He picked me up from the bed like an adult would to a small kid and placed me on a huge chair, kind of one found at the salon which sat in front of a huge wooden framed mirror.

"Woah!" I squealed.

He laughed and went inside the closet to get his coat.

The girl, Deborah started combing my hair into different sections. Something got trapped within the comb from my hair causing me to yelp.

Fyodor peeked out again. "Is everything alright?"

"There's dried blood in her hair. She needs to shower," she said in a dangerous voice. If she were a knife, I would have been stabbed by then already.

She did not sound Russian at all.

I looked at Fyodor for a moment and got down off the chair.

"You should get your stuff done. I'll go shower first," I said smiling.

I grabbed the package which had my dress and walked into the bathroom locking myself in.

I finished my ablutions and finished showering. I used his body wash and shampoo. There were tons of other things but I did not know their use so I left them alone.

He had a huge ass bathroom, big enough for ten people to fit in comfortably.

I grabbed a dry towel from one of the hangers and dried myself. Pulling out the garment from the package he had handed me earlier, I felt the smooth fabric come in contact with my fingers. Turned out it was a beautiful white dress with red floral print.

I put it on to find it was reaching down a bit below my knees and the sleeves went to my wrists. The cold shoulders made me feel like a princess. I could not help but twirl and jump once giggling to myself.

I smiled at myself pulling out a choker with red roses which went well with my dress. I put it on walking out of the bathroom tidying down the bottom layers.

I saw him sitting on his bed, his eyes widening at me causing me to blush.

"You look so pretty!" He said grinning. "Awww look at you, you're blushing," he laughed.

I walked to the chair and sat on it not to keep Deborah watch us being silly.

She plugged in the dryer and dried my hair, preparing to cut it and style.

She put a huge plastic apron like thing around me, fastening it with a velcro flap around my head and I could feel her cutting my hair, her long sharp black nails somewhat scaring me.

Those are some natural self-defense stuff women tend to keep.

It took her quite a while to transform me from an ugly cavewoman to a human being.

I could hear Fyodor occasionally giggling when I let out a cry of pain every time she hurt me while waxing off my face and legs.

After she was done and left, I walked to him and slapped him playfully on his arm. "You're so cruel," I said laughing.

He flinched and grabbed his arm, hissing out as if in pain.

"Oh my god, did it hurt that bad?" I asked my face bearing the expression of confusion and concern.

He grabbed me by the waist smirking, pulling me closer to him.

My mouth was wide open in shock.

"You're such a good actor! I'm amazed," I said bursting into laughter while he laughed as well.

Our laughter faded away and I saw his face turn serious, his gaze flicking between my eyes and lips.

I felt my mouth and throat dry and my heart in chaos.

I don't think I'm ready for this.

But something inside me wanted me to go for it.

He had almost closed his eyes, our lips almost touching when Artyom blurted in.

He was staring at us with wide eyes and an open mouth, all frozen while he let go of me and I looked down at my bare feet all flushed and embarrassed.

He coughed and put the huge tray of breakfast on the bed and walked away swiftly.

"Um...you should eat some breakfast," he said. "And your shoes are in my closet."

Oof awkward.

"You should eat too," I said. He often skipped breakfast and all he ate was that soup and bread.

"Nah," he said ignoring casually.

I held his hand tight. I did not want to force him or get him angry. Most importantly, I did not want to make him feel that I was taking advantage of what I was to him and that I was trying to change him into something else.

"I'm just...not used to," he said.

"It's just eating," I said laughing. "I wanna share my food you know," I said tugging at his sleeves.

"But...I don't really eat all that stuff," he said looking at the plate of red velvet cake, eggs, and toast.

"Come on!" I groaned.

"It's meant for one person," he said laughing.

"We will share, okay?" I said shrugging.

"Fine..." He mumbled as he sat across the other side of the plate.

I look at the plate of food. There was only one knife and fork each. We looked at each other in confusion.

"Um...you could feed me..." I said opening my mouth. He chuckled cutting the toast and the egg and feeding it to me.

"It's really good!" I exclaimed throwing my hands into the air making him laugh.

I looked at him eagerly as he ingested a morsel himself, making me clap in happiness.

I saw him chewing on the food nervously but finally gulping.

"How is it?" I asked him leaning down and peeking up at him.

"It's really good," he said smiling. "I missed this..."

"Why do you eat only soup and bread?"

"My body couldn't take in anything else after...what happened so I was afraid to eat anything else. But now surprisingly, I don't feel bad at all," he said smiling.

"That's great," I said smiling big.

Fyodor took me out to the orchards at the back of the house that day. The day was windy as usual. I could feel the wind against my face and my skirt fluttering against the direction I was walking in.

This was the best day of my life.

For the first time, I felt that I had no worries in the world.

The first time my heavy head felt light.

The first time I felt happiness, the real happiness.

The first time I smiled when I felt like it.

The first time when I felt that I had everything that I needed.

The first time when everything was going right...just the way I had dreamt of...

He had his arms around my shoulders while our feet trod on the soft grass below our shoes. I could see the whole back side of the residence which looked huge.

It seemed weird how earlier; I used to beg the day to be over fast while now I was complaining about how fast the day was passing by.

I laughed at his silly jokes, indulging ourselves in a friendly banter and acting like two stupid people.

The day seemed bright and cheerful, the birds chirping while the larks sang. I saw tons of butterflies around in the flower garden, taking my thoughts back to the day when the principal had scolded me...

Don't think about the past. It will hurt.

He showed me around the area where they grew fruits telling me something or the other about each of them. The air emanated a sweet, fruity fragrance. The whole place felt like heaven to me.

I saw him walking to a rose bush while I followed. He carefully plucked a rose and offered it to me, giving me a kiss on the cheek making me smile.

He looked like a five-year-old giving something to his newly found crush at school. It looked nothing like the movies or books but it did carry a genuine feeling, something which melted me from the inside filling me with an unknown warmth. I felt feverish but in a good way.

I knew I just wanted him. No, pardon me, I NEEDED him. He seemed to be the clean and fresh air that I had wanted to breathe for so long.

At times he did act clumsy.

So did I.

He was inexperienced.

So was I.

We were both new to this feeling. At moments it felt so good, so good that it was difficult for me to accept that it was true.

This is too good to be true...

If this lasts forever, I would need nothing else to survive on.

It was late afternoon when he walked me down the brick pavement to a small outdoor table which was filled with food condiments of all sorts.

I realized that we had not eaten lunch, not that I needed it that day. I was too occupied spending time with him that I had forgotten about everything else.

Ever really felt the way you feel when something absolutely amazing happens to you?

Your stomach is filled with excitement, your mind too occupied to think about anything else.

This was just the case for me.

His love was more than enough for me to keep me alive. I felt as if I did not need anything else ever.

"I'm really not hungry, my stomach is oddly full," I said to him.

He chuckled.

"I can't let your tummy go hungry," he said poking my stomach making me giggle. He held my wrist and dragged me to the table, making me sit on a chair, making me sit before joining me.

There was a huge array of fruits there, mostly berries. I saw a woman walking towards us with a tray which had a huge pie in it.

"You really did not have to do any of this you know," I said pouting.

"But you know I will," he said laughing.

I rolled my eyes while the lady served me a slice of pie, the beautiful smell taking over my senses.

"Thank you!" I chirped at her. I saw her eyeing at his plate looking confused while he went back to his grumpy state refusing to ask for a slice. The lady looked scared.

I giggled and placed my plate in front of him while taking his empty one and placing in front of me.

"Can I get a slice please?" I asked the lady.

Looking confused, she cut and placed another slice on my plate. I looked at her walk away quickly as Fyodor sneered at her.

"Why do you have to be so mean to her?" I asked giving him a disappointed look.

He looked at me like an angry kid. He smiled at me seeing me laugh.

I smiled and took a bite, the pastry melted in my mouth leaving behind a trail of the sweet sour filling.

"What is the filling made up of?"

"Vladimir cherries, isn't it really good?" He asked looking happy.

"Yush," I said my mouth filled with food which sent him over the edge of laughing while I sat there looking like a puffer fish.

He made me eat the Astrakhan watermelon that they grew, which was so tasty.

We ate a full range of raspberries, wild strawberries, blueberries and something they called Malina, which looked like a faded version of raspberry. We even had cranberries and a whole range of cheeses.

We laughed and spent a lot of time together till it was evening. We were just entering the house when he got a call. I heard him talk to someone in Russian. I could see his face turn into that of confusion and anger.

"Is everything alright?" I asked him squeezing his right shoulder.

"Just go inside," he said almost growling.

My face drooped down like a dead sunflower. It felt really sad seeing him like that. He was a whole different person that day and...

Now he is back to his original self.....

Planning

I entered the house to see Artyom standing near the door. "Here to escort you," he said. He looked serious as well, in no mood to joke or fool around.

"What happened though?" I asked following his fast paces.

"The healing antidotes got stolen, and all the employees are getting suspicious that you've stolen it."

"But I was with him the entire time!" I said trying to defend myself.

"They're just saying because you were the only supposed captive out there."

I kept shut.

He opened the door and opened the bed, leading me to the basement.

"I had a question."

"What is it?"

I entered the basement. I walked into the room to find Edvin and Shandrel sleeping in the bunker beds. It was painful to see them. They were all sick and bloody.

I felt guilty.

Guilty that they had been here, while I had been out there having fun.

I saw Dasha come into the room with two small bottles of some substance. She stopped right in her tracks when she saw me. She hid the bottles behind her.

"What are you doing here?" She asked feeling threatened.

"Am I not supposed to be here? Besides what are you hiding?" I asked her raising an eyebrow.

Were those the bottles of the healing antidote?

She aimed her gun at me. As brave as she was trying to portray herself, I could see her hands were trembling. The beads of sweat were clearly visible on her forehead.

"You can just tell me and then kill me," I said to her dryly.

I looked behind to them, "But just take care of these two people. None of them deserves any of these." I said looking back at the red haired widow.

She ran to me and hugged me breaking down.

"I...I stole the antidotes," she sobbed, her voice breaking. "Please help me! I can't let their parents suffer from the loss of their kids. I know how it feels," she said crying harder.

I looked at those bottles for a long period of time.

This was wrong, yet right.

He had hurt them; it was just fair to have them cured. But at the same time they were stolen. But then he would never have had given them away.

I took the bottles from her hand and walked to the bunker beds. I opened the cap, lifting the sheets off them and poured it on top of their wounds. She stood behind me watching them with curiosity. I was confident it would work on them. Seconds ticked off but nothing happened.

I looked up at her.

"Are you sure it is the antidote?" I asked her sternly.

"I think so..." She said unsure.

"You 'think' so? Are you out of your fucking mind? What if it's a wrong...?"

"Look," she said, her glassy eyes turning wide at them.

I turned to look at them. I could see the injured parts being replaced with new cells and skin. New strands of hair growing out of the injured cracks as they healed.

I looked at them, wishing they would wake up soon. My heart

was beating fast. I was looking at them with anticipation. Every cell of mine wished they would wake up soon or at least we would get some signal that they were going to wake up.

My heart was fluttering wildly, just like a lifeless leaf on a cold autumn evening. I had almost given up and was on the verge of tears when Shandrel's hand moved a little.

Dasha leaped up with joy.

"He is alright! He is waking up!" She said in shaking excitement.

Our eyes moved to Edvin who lay just like that. I saw Dasha checking his pulse and breath, her face going pale.

"Is he alright?" I asked her concerned and scared.

"He seems...dead," she mumbled.

I was scared. It was news of double trouble. It would be earth-shattering news if Edvin was dead, and more trouble would follow if traces of the stolen antidote were found on his body. His exterior seemed to have healed completely so I could not really understand what could have gone wrong on the insides.

I sat by his side covering my face with my palms thinking of any other way which could save us all from any following disaster.

Dasha was leaning against the wall sobbing and tensed.

"Hey..." We heard a groan.

We looked behind me to find a pair of bright green eyes which belonged to Edvin.

I sighed in relief. Dasha rushed by his side happily.

"Are you alright?" She asked him stroking his hair.

"I...I am," he said with a hoarse voice trying to get up.

While Dasha was tending to Edvin, I looked at Shandrel.

His chest was heaving up and down gently as if he was sleeping.

I went closer to him and whispered near his ear, "Are you okay?"

He opened his large eyelids and gave me a strange look.

"Water," he managed to say in a gruff voice.

Dasha was looking at us and immediately rushed to the kitchen to get water.

Edvin was trying to get up. I gave him a hand with it and

made him sit against the headboard. Dasha ran in and helped Shandrel up. She made him drink some of the life saving liquid. She had even brought a glass for Edvin.

As happy she looked, I could figure out that she was dying from the inside. Maybe she was still mourning for her husband and her newborn. Whereas it was difficult for me to accept that Fyodor was the reason that her life was in disarray. He, himself had been through a lot which made him the way he was. Maybe it is never anyone's fault. It's just the situation which frames people the way they are unless they choose to start a storm themselves. Or they may even choose to change themselves. But then people have their own philosophies so we cannot really do anything but try cope or fight back.

Edvin was lost in his thoughts.

"How long was I out for?" Shandrel asked.

"Six days," she answered.

"It can't be…" Edvin said trailing off, looking at himself. "It hurt a lot, I could not have gotten well in such a less amount of time," he said looking at me.

"Long story," I replied.

"We have time," Shandrel said and Edvin looked at me with curiosity.

"Dasha stole a healing antidote to quicken your healing," I replied.

"Such medicines don't exist," Shandrel said.

"He is making them and testing on us, isn't he?" Edvin asked.

I nodded my head in affirmation.

"Why is she helping us? Isn't she suppose to work for him?" Edvin threw a nasty look at Dasha.

"Fyodor killed her family…" I trailed off.

Shandrel looked angry but paused looking at me dressed like this. "Why have you dressed up like this?"

I felt guilt kicking in again.

"I was given such a treatment because it's my birthday today," I lied.

"I don't want your parents to go through what I did, especially when they did nothing of the sort to deserve this. I will help you escape and go back to your homes," she said boldly.

I looked at Dasha.

"What if we are caught?" Edvin asked looking devastated. He had given up hope. His face looked drained of energy and peace.

"I have a plan," she said.

I kept quiet.

"Just give me a moment," she said dragging me out of the room.

"Look, I know you love him, I'm running away with these kids and I know you can't. These kids deserve a better life, they can't stay here," she said tearing up a bit.

I looked behind to what had happened that day. I could feel few tears drop down my cheek. I could not let Shandrel and Edvin die or live like this. I wanted to help, but it wouldn't happen without going against Fyodor.

Or maybe I could just cut my feelings off before they grew more.

"Count me in," I said.

"What?" She said. "You were on a date with him, you love him… you can't…"

"Why don't you say that you don't trust me?" I asked giving her a serious look.

She looked at me for a while. "Fine...I don't trust you…You'll spill everything to him and we will be in trouble or could even lose our lives."

"When are you leaving?" I asked.

"Tomorrow morning," she said.

"I'll escape with you," I said.

"What? No! You can't," she said shaking my shoulders. "You have to help him."

"I won't be able to forgive myself if something happened to you, please! Let me help! Please..." I begged.

Every cell of mine screamed at me to take my words back

but this situation was as such, I could not have risked these innocent people for the love I had desired for.

"What if the plan fails?" I asked.

Dasha still looked hesitant to take me in. I bet she was regretting saying that in front of me. It was clear that she had meant to escape with them leaving me behind.

I shook my head and walked into the room to check up on them but I was glad that they were sitting up feeling a bit eased.

"There's only one plan to get out. We really don't have a plan B. It's a do or die situation. We can't really afford to lose this time." Dasha said her face dropping down.

There was an eerie silence.

"We can do this, guys," I said trying my best to flash an encouraging smile.

"Yes," Shandrel said looking thoughtful.

"What if someone walks down in here and discovers all that has happened now?" Edvin asked.

I looked at Dasha since I was clueless about this too.

"They won't. I've been given charge of this and beside, this is not going as per planning," she said.

"What do you mean?" I asked.

"I really don't know. Things are very lenient. He thinks more about you than concentrating on what he is supposed to do. He never hesitates to kill anyone but he spares you each and every time which is shocking," she looked at me.

"What if she betrays us?" Shandrel asked giving me a dirty look. "We heard everything, you're with him. I saw how he carried you with worry written all over his face before conducting that on us. He was with you for an entire hour," he said in a voice laced with distrust.

"He has hurt me enough. If he cared about me, he would never have hurt me this way," I said tearing up. "I don't trust him."

A part of me felt guilty of telling this to them. A part of my heart felt really horrible to be backstabbing him and plotting behind his back.

"You like him back, don't you?" Dasha asked smiling sadly and squeezing my shoulder a bit.

I do.

I love him more than I had ever loved anything...

All the moments flashed in front of the eyes.

The hugs, the kisses, the cuddles and most importantly...the smile.....his smile...

I couldn't help but let down tears.

"I do love him... a part of me cares for him. I want to show him the brighter side of life. I want to take away his grumpy side and replace it with happiness. I just want him to show what love, happiness, care is and how positive life could be. But I guess we are in too much of darkness to see the light anymore."

I couldn't believe I was pulling in the darkness and pushing the light away from my life.

Everyone was silent.

"He cares a lot for you too. He spent hours organizing what you saw in the afternoon, all handpicked by him. He needs you," she said sighing. "You can walk out of this now if you want. But I beg you to keep this a secret, not for you but these two kids," she looked at me with pleading eyes. "We won't tell the cops. I will just leave these kids to where they belong and vanish somewhere else."

Even if that all had happened, there was still a bit of doubt lingering in a corner of my mind.

What if he hurts me when they leave?

It was true that he had cared for me when I was hurt, but it was never a situation when he had tried not to inflict any kind of pain on me.

"I will say I ran away and frame some reason," Edvin said.

"So will I, just for your sake," Shandrel said.

I laughed.

"You people are delusional!" I exclaimed.

They threw me a weird look.

"I'm staying with you people and we all are escaping together.

Lives are more important than love, is what I believe. I'm with you." I said.

"Are you sure?" Dasha asked me looking concerned.

Even if I wanted something else, I nodded my head. Shandrel and Edvin going back home was more important than my love story with Fyodor. I wished I had more time with him but maybe it was destined to be an unopened chapter of our lives, folded and kept away, never to be read.

I looked down at my hand thinking of his face for a second but made up my mind.

"Justice and fairness means more to me than anything else," I said. "Tell us the plan," I looked up at Dasha.

She hugged me tight and I saw Edvin smiling whereas Shandrel shot me a grin.

"You will get to the light of your life, you deserve it," Shandrel said.

"True," Dasha said.

"What's the plan?" Edvin asked.

Dasha spent the next forty minutes describing the plan to us and clearing our queries. It sounded risky indeed.

"Are you sure this will work out?" Edvin asked.

"I'm scared," Shandrel said.

"Yeah, we can easily get caught." I sighed.

"Come on guys, at least we can try! Don't you trust me?" She asked.

"We do but…" Shandrel said. He looked clearly disheartened.

"We have to trust her. We have no other way," I said in a matter of fact voice.

"You're right," Edvin said.

"Mhm," mumbled Shandrel.

We were surprised to hear somebody walking down the stairs. Edvin and Shandrel quickly got into their sheets and pretended like sleeping as Dasha ran out of the bedroom to see who it was. I gathered the empty antidote bottles and hid it in under the mattress and hid behind the bedroom wall to see who it was. Surprisingly, it was Daniil talking to Dasha.

He must have been frustrated and angered by what had happened.

Dasha responded positive to what he said before he started asking where I was and tried walking past her to enter the bedroom to find me. Getting him anywhere near the bedroom could prove risky and troublesome, so I walked out myself to greet him.

"Here I am," I said making a straight face.

"Where are the boys?" He said trying to walk past me.

I stood in front of him getting into his way when he shot me a suspicious look.

"They're resting after the experiment, you dumbhead. Don't make noise and disturb them. You will be at fault if something bad happens. You don't want that, do you?" I asked him sternly in a low voice.

He looked at me for a moment and he knew not to go or disturb in a domain which he was not related to, else he could be killed.

He gave me a defeated look and walked past Dasha up the stairs. We saw him go out of the basement.

I was about to open my mouth to say something when she shushed me.

She kept me like that for about five minutes after which she came near to my ears and said that we would talk by whispering and that we could not risk getting caught.

I saw that Shandrel and Edvin had gotten up looking at each other. She walked to them and asked them to whisper talk as well.

"We are leaving tomorrow," she said going to the kitchen.

"Yes, we are," I agreed.

"Everybody will be distracted and busy arranging for the stuff for the picnic and that is when we slip," she said serving some kind of soup in four little bowls and adding spoons to them.

"Ask them if they need bread with soup," she asked.

I went to the bedroom and asked them if they needed some to which they said yes.

I went back to the kitchen to pass on what they had said. She placed two slices of cheesy garlic bread on each soup plate. I helped her carry two bowls while she walked behind me holding two more plates.

I gave each of them their bowls while I sat on a chair right next to Edvin's bed. Dasha held her bowl in one hand and was using her other hand to eat.

"The journey will be long. We might not get to eat much. We may have to skip meals if the need arises. So eat quick and well," she said.

We finished our meals and washed. It was a subject of great delight to see that Edvin and Shandrel were walking around normal.

Fyodor had to be a genius.

I could not help but smile at how intelligent he was. I slid my hands into the apron and felt the empty bottle of the antidote. This would be the last evidence of him in my life besides the memories I had. I had fallen for him, yes I had. And I could not lie to the fact, even to myself. Maybe it would all fade by passing time. And then at last, there would only remain a fact that I once had fallen for such a man. If I managed to escape successfully, I may not even see him again.

"Hey," Dasha said tapping my back.

"Yes?"

"You cannot risk telling about this to anybody else, not even Alyosha," she said.

"I know," I kept silent for a while. "I want her away from this violence as much as possible. Can't really let her know."

Honestly I was scared. What if they tortured her to dig any information out of her, thinking if she knew anything about it?

"I have a question," I asked Dasha.

"What is it?"

"What if they trouble her regarding my disappearance? They

all know we are good friends beside we have had our share of alone time," I asked her.

"Artyom will never let her get killed. He will not even let anyone lay a finger on her. He is that possessive of her," she said.

"But the man in power is Fyodor. You never really know what he will do," I said worried.

"Fyodor cares a lot for his brother and what he wants. The thing for which you worry about will never happen. They will not lay a finger on Alyosha even if she kills someone. She means a lot to Artyom and she is capable of getting away with whatever she does. She chooses to be a dutiful maid instead of being a spoiled brat, that's her choice. That is why she is respected by everyone around here," she stated.

This was a major risk we all were taking. A single mistake and we all would die.

Doing all of this behind his back, I did not even deserve forgiveness or mercy.

"Now you better go to bed," she said gesturing me to the bathroom.

As I had seen Boris do, Alyosha pressed a tile and the old metal door came to view. It slid to reveal my old bedroom. I went in and heard the door closing behind me. I turned behind me to see Dasha's face one last time that night.

"Goodnight," was all that she said before the door shut close before her.

I had grown tired from our sweet adventure. I climbed onto the bed and stared at the ceiling, my eyes occasionally drooping. Unsatisfied with my sleeping posture, I turned down on my stomach where the huge cupboard came to my vision.

I wish I had his arms around me...

The smell of his sweet cologne...

As eager I was to explore what was inside, I was very tired. Before I knew anything I passed out into a deep dark void, the sweet memories of the day flooding my mind.

Surrender

My eyelids fluttered open to an empty and silent room. I wished I could go back twenty four hours before...

I was still clad in the same clothes, the choker and shoes still on. I had been too lazy to take them off. I was sure my face was a mess.

I craved for an open window, birds chirping, flowers dancing to the tune of the breeze and the sunlight greeting me. I had closed my eyes again to get a bit more of sleep when I heard the sensor equipped doors open and saw Dasha rushing to me to wake me up.

"You're already late!" She screeched.

All the plans that we had managed to make came rushing to me.

Shit!

I ran out of the opened door to the bathroom which was luckily at the outside.

"I'm getting ready! Don't come in!" I yelled hurriedly.

I showered and brushed my teeth and finished all of my daily ablutions.

My mind was constantly busy thinking about how we would escape safely without getting caught.

"Are you done?" Dasha yelled.

"Just give me two minutes!" I shouted from the bathroom.

"Quick!" She said in a commanding voice.

I looked at the dress he had bought for me laying on the bathroom floor.

I wish I could take it with me...

Snapping out of my thoughts, I dried myself with a used towel that was already there. It barely helped but I had no time to judge. I pulled my drawer and randomly pulled out a pair of pants and a baggy t-shirt along with a pair of fresh inner garments. I wore them as quickly as I could. The lower part of my pants got wet from the wet bathroom floor but I knew it would dry later. I hurriedly left the bathroom barely escaping from slipping on the slippery bathroom floor.

When I entered the hidden room, Dasha ran out to open the bathroom door and gestured Shandrel and Edvin to come in quickly.

We all were curious to see where the hidden tunnel was, through which we were to escape.

"How many secret doors are there in here?" I asked.

"That's a secret," Dasha said smirking.

I could not help but laugh a bit.

We all got into the room and Dasha opened a cabinet at the right side of the room which revealed a sailor wheel like object.

"What the hell is that?" I asked.

"A master lock," she said. "It will take them hours to break this and get in here if they ever figure out we have escaped through the secret passage in this room."

"Where is the secret passage?" Edvin asked.

"Why are you locking us in this room?" Shandrel asked.

"You will see," was all what she said.

She pressed some switch which closed the metal door shut, leaving us trapped in the room where I slept for the night. I saw red lights all around the wheel and low beeping noises.

"Won't they get notified if you're using the master lock?" I asked. "I mean, every device is computer generated, they would know."

"They have disabled the lock alarms in certain parts of the

house. As far as I know this is disabled too. I'm not a fool to use this, you know." She said.

She rotated the wheel three times and the last time she did, we could hear the faint noises of gears rotating and some mechanism clicking together. It made me feel as if something was clasping against each other locking the door real secure and tight.

She locked the cabinet and took a deep breath.

"Where is the secret tunnel?" Shandrel asked.

I could see they were eager to escape. Who wouldn't be? Any prisoner would escape if given even a little chance, especially when there was a question of life and death.

Dasha went to the huge wardrobe looking thing which I had always wanted to explore, opening it totally.

I hadn't been able to think that there could be an escape passage this way.

I walked in there.

Huge built in shelves decorated either side of the walls, filled with old books, mostly of which looked like old records. They were dust laden and half of them looked yellow and moth eaten. I could see cobwebs at the corners. There was no lighting and I could see that the place had not been cleaned since ages.

We were about to travel a long distance and I thought nothing could be better than having a book to keep me company. A few piles of thick leather bound books caught my attention. I picked the topmost one and followed Dasha. We walked a few steps and stopped in front of a wooden door.

"Please don't tell me this is the end," Edvin said.

"Of course not," Dasha said with a tinge of annoyance in her voice.

She opened the panel of a small box setup on the wall to reveal another biometric device. She pressed her finger against the screen and the door unlocked to reveal another passageway.

"What's the time now?" I asked her.

"It's nine in the morning already," she said.

We were running behind the time by half an hour. I went to work around ten. A minute late, and they would come down to fetch me and everything would blow up. So we had to leave as soon as possible, so that we could travel as far as we could without being in the risk of getting caught.

"We have to hurry," Shandrel said.

"Quick, get in," Dasha said motioning us to get into the passageway. I went in while the others followed.

Dasha got in locking the door behind us and we were drowned in darkness. I heard Dasha slapping her hands on the wall, perhaps searching for something.

I heard something click, sounded like a switch.

I saw small yellow bulbs flickering on and lighting the entire hallway. It was a dome shaped tunnel which looked very old. The ground I saw was dusty. Seemed like no one had swept it from the time it was built.

"Hurry!" Dasha said getting in front of us and leading the way. We followed her for about fifteen minutes into a never ending passageway.

Shandrel groaned, "How long do we have to walk for?"

"A bit more," Dasha said.

We might have walked for around a few seconds more when we saw a flight of stairs.

"This is it," she said.

There were no barricades on either side of the stairs but I did not complain since the stairs were wide enough for us to not fall off.

We hauled ourselves up the stairs with our aching limbs.

"It's already nine thirty! We have to be quick," Dasha said in order to motivate us.

Dasha opened another blue coloured, rusty metal door through the biometric device.

"Why is there biometric device on like every door?" Edvin asked.

"Security reasons," Dasha said.

We walked out of the door into a small space which looked really dark after the metal door closed by itself.

"Ouch," I heard Edvin say after hearing a thud.

"Are you alright?" Shandrel asked.

We were supposed to be in the garage at the backyard.

I heard someone jumping.

"The keys…" Dasha said. She was trying hard to get the keys of the car perhaps.

"Get it quick!" I said.

I heard something falling to the ground.

"Got it," Dasha said huffing.

I could hear her footsteps. She was walking away from us.

I could hear something unbolt. I saw a crack of light which was getting bigger bigger till the entire garage door was opened.

Dasha unlocked the car which looked like a mustang and got into it. I opened the front door and got in too while those two got in, at the back.

Dasha switched on the ignition.

"Ready?" She said.

"Yes!" We all yelled in unison.

She got the car out of the garage and revved up the engine.

Now this was a serious part. We were mentally praying that no one saw us. We were about to take the road which went beside the orchard at the back of the house and into the woods.

I was told that there was no boundary of the house where the orchard was so getting into the woods and taking the highway from there to Petrozavodsk airport was not a problem.

"Put your seatbelts on. You never know when I'll have to speed up in case somebody sees us," Dasha said.

I put on my seatbelt and looked behind us to see that they had done the same.

"Let's go," Edvin said.

Dasha revved up the engine and started driving.

Could this be the road to freedom?

Will I really escape?

Will I really be free?

My eyes welled up with tears. A part of me was regretting this decision. I knew I would never see him again.

His beautiful heterochromic eyes.

Our fights.

Our love.

All gone.

I saw the stretch of the green grass ahead of us. It was only yesterday that we were walking on them being so close to each other and now...

I had tears welled up in my eyes since I had been in the shower. I was trying hard to hold them back.

Maybe Dasha saw this.

"I know it hurts but it was your choice, after all," she said.

"I know..."

I looked at the rear mirror and saw them looking outside at the orange trees while the sun shone brightly at their faces which barely bothered them. There were small smiles on their faces.

I could still see the table there beside the brick pavement where we had eaten the day before.

A few tears rolled down my cheek.

I'm so sorry...

I didn't mean to hurt you this way...

But this needs to be done...

Their smiles were more important to me than my stupid adventure.

"This was a smooth escape," she said pulling up the car on the smooth road from the bumpy soil.

"You better pray they don't come up smarter than us," I said.

Fyodor was unpredictable. You never know when he was up with a trick up his sleeve. I did not want to be deceived while in the process of deceiving him.

We had been driving for the past fifteen minutes when I saw

small black huts facing river Onega.

"Who lives in such houses?" Shandrel asked scrunching up his nose.

"This is the ghost town Pegrema is famous for. People don't live here. This village was destroyed during the Russian revolution." Dasha said.

I looked out at the breathtaking scenery we passed across.

"There's even a chapel," Edvin said.

"That's the Varlaam Khutynsky chapel. It was built in the 1770s. They've removed all the artifacts from inside it," she said driving calmly.

We had been driving for about five hours by the countryside. I had been reading the book that I had managed to get from the wardrobe. Turned out it was not even a book. It was Fyodor's diary after all when he was seventeen. It was difficult for me to imagine that such a violent man used to be such a loving and kind person once. There were chapters that he had written about his crush, a girl named Tanya Grey. I never knew he had such artistic talents. He had sketched beautiful pictures of a girl. Maybe those were the pictures of Tanya Grey. I could not help but tear up. The last entry was him being very excited of meeting her dad and then there was nothing.

What had happened to such a beautiful person?

Who damaged him like this?

Why does he kill?

I was lost in my thoughts when Dasha pulled up at a spot where we saw a party going at an empty area by the road.

"Some kind of mass picnic is going on," Edvin said. "Or a party maybe."

"I'm hungry," Shandrel said.

"I can sneak some food for you if you want," she said.

I looked out of the window and observed what was going on properly.

There was a line of vans by the street. People were bringing out trays of food and placing them on the huge tables decorated with festoons and balloons in the field. It seemed like an outdoor food party of some sort.

I was nearly blind for not having used spectacles for long.

I heard a loud gun shot in the car.

I was shocked. I gasped and looked back to see an injured Edvin gasping and convulsing as blood poured out from his mouth.

"What the fuck just happened?" I yelled.

Dasha and Shandrel were too shocked to respond.

"That's him!" Dasha yelled trying to start the car but it didn't.

Edvin looked like a gasping fish in need of water, when he needed air.

"Do something!" I yelled at Dasha nearly in tears.

Everything felt as if it was fading away. All the hard work crashing down to nothing but shards of broken glass.

I felt something cold press against my temple making me gasp.

The familiar cologne.

The same voice.

"Hello there, darling," he said chuckling.

The warmth had vanished...

The same cold demeanor.

Fyodor had found me.

He had won in the cat mice chase.

"Oh Dasha, I never expected this from you. You must be really a fool to think that we had disabled the equipments," he said in his low voice. "It seems you've been trying hard to join your family up in heaven."

"She was just trying to help," I said in her defense.

"Shush honey," he said gritting his teeth pressing the metal gun against my temple harder making me flinch.

Out of nowhere in the serious atmosphere, Shandrel got out of the car and started running. Fyodor took his head out of the car window and shot thrice.

"Why are you doing this?" I asked.

His face looked cold and hard. All that had happened seemed

like a distant dream...as if it had never happened...

He opened the side of my car door and pulled me out. He had my head in a deadlock which made it difficult for me to breath. He leaned down to my ears and whispered, "Have I not done enough for you?"

"I never asked you to." I said bluntly.

"An ungrateful little minx, aren't you?" He said almost growling and sending chills down my spine.

"I am!" I yelled at his face.

He kept quiet for a moment.

I felt a severing pain when he dragged me back to his car by my hair. No amount of yelping or crying made him change his mind.

He pushed me at the front seat of my car, chaining me and locked me up at my back.

It was difficult to imagine that the person whom I was reading about in the diary, with whom I had spent the most beautiful moments of my life till this moment of existence, and the person with whom I was dealing at the present were the same.

I heard him opening the door and getting behind the wheel.

"What you're doing is wrong," I said. "I tried to make you understand."

"You should have thought about this before running away," he said staring coldly at his wheel.

He ignored what I was saying and started the ignition. I saw Shandrel's body lying on the road.

"What if you had a child and this happened to him?" I asked.

"I wouldn't care," he replied his eyes fixed to the road.

"Of course you would! That would be your kid! Why do you have to kill?" I shouted.

"Do you want me to duct tape your mouth?" He yelled at me.

I kept quiet.

I did not know what to think.

It was already dark when we were nearing the hell hole.

"You have to let go of her," I mumbled.

He stopped the car and looked at me.

"Let go of who?" He asked looking at me.

"Tanya Grey," I said boldly. "Artyom told me that her father called you names but that doesn't mean you will kill people who anger you. And for the experiments, what you're doing is wrong. You're snatching people away from their families. That's something you have no right over, especially when they're innocent and have done you no wrong."

Even if there were no lights, I could see his cheeks glistening. His racking sobs filled the entire car.

"I did not want to lose her. She meant the world to me. We had promised to be together no matter what, but she walked away. I could not wake up from that ever since. My dad never cared for me. I never got to know my mom. It is not my fault my dad ended up with me from a prostitute. And it hurts when people call me a son of a whore and such."

"I had let her go when I met you. Never in my wildest dreams had I thought you'd bring in such a change in me. But then when you left...I just couldn't..."

We kept quiet for a few minutes before I broke the silence.

"My life has been terrible too. But that does not mean you have to hurt others for what happens to you. And I'm sorry for running away...I was just trying to help Dasha...But you should have not killed them..."

"Killing has become an addiction for me," he admitted.

"I can see that well." I said.

"And when I saw you vanished with them, I thought you turned against me or left me for good."

I could not help but blush.

"I fell for you..." I said trailing off. "Even if you had told me not to."

"I...I...um..." He said fumbling and searching for words.

I looked up at him and I could see him shaking and shivering a bit.

"I love you and I don't think I can ever change into a good man without you," he blurted out. "And I'm ready..."

I could feel my face getting red and hot which made him chuckle and smile.

I had missed this...

"Ready for what?"

"For repentance...for surrender...Artyom has already called the cops..." He said looking down at his fingers.

He was changing...for real...

"You know you have me with you no matter what...I'll never stop loving you..."

He came closer to me, it seemed like he was hesitating for some reason.

He looked around while I was sitting there wondering what he was planning on doing. He pulled out the key to the lock which bound the chain around me and unlocked it.

I could hear the faint sound of the sirens at a distance.

But nonetheless, we kept sitting there staring into each other's eyes as if we had an eternity.

"I wish I could see your eyes once again," I said gazing into his brown lens clad eyes.

"I wish I could hug you one more time," he said.

We both knew he could have taken off his lenses and he could have hugged me for all he could, but decided to sit down like that and gaze at each other, taking in all that we could.

It was as if I could feel the synchronizing universe around me. I could feel the breeze blowing outside, the crickets chirping in the dark night while the stars twinkled above in the night sky.

The sound of the sirens was getting louder and louder each passing moment.

"I hope we meet again," I said.

"This is not a goodbye," he said.

"I wish we had more time."

"We will have plenty of time, trust me."

The sirens of the police vehicle could not get any louder.

"To a better future," he said.

"To a better future," I mumbled.

A few Russian policemen were talking to each other in loud voices. Their voices grew louder and louder till two of them opened the car door and pulled him out of his car and ordered me to get out.

I got out of the car. Some lady cops draped a tweed coat around me. I was seen as a victim of his operations. But for some reason I was calm, quiet, and a bit sad too. I had found a place for him in my heart even after what he did. I believe every human being must be given a chance, and he had provided his share of proving himself to me. I had forgiven him.

Many would think I am stupid to have let go of him that easy. But I considered myself honoured, that I could change such a man.

My reward?

That he changed. He was that brave to surrender than to shut me up and run away. And I will always be proud of him for that.

I kept looking at him when he was being dragged away by the cops. He gave me one last look before was shoved inside the vehicle and driven away.

"I'll always love and respect you for what you did. You shall always be remembered," I whispered to myself. "You're my hero."

After Nine Years

"I've fixed a date for you!" Melissa said hugging me tight from the behind squealing.

"Not again, Mel," I said sighing.

She had been trying so hard to set me up with some guy, but every time I go on a date, something or the other just blows up and everything turns into a major disaster.

"But he's a Russian! And he is so hot!" She said fanning herself which made me laugh.

Fyodor would have been thirty by now.

My laugh just faded away.

Melissa understood why.

"You can't wait for him forever," she said in an understanding voice.

"You don't understand!" I said frustrated. "Every time I go to see a guy, his image pops in my mind."

It was true. He was still there in my heart, the memory of him getting into the van still very fresh in my mind. It seemed as if it was just yesterday.

His twenty-year-old self looking at me for the last time we saw each other.

That haunted me...

"It's been nine years..." She said sighing. "You can't go on being like this."

"I can't move on either way." I said tearing up.

"Look, I've already fixed your date with him and he is so eager to meet you," she tried convincing me to go.

"Let's just go to the spa and hang out. How about that?" I asked her.

"Um, this may sound weird but," she stopped in mid-sentence.

"But what?" I looked up at her from my papers.

"This guy actually paid Bryan two thousand bucks so that he could meet you. He was literally on his knees." She said.

"Now that makes things even creepier, Melissa! Why would you set up such a guy for me?" I asked bewildered and shocked, throwing my pen away.

"I don't know! Bryan never wanted the money. He just forced him!" She said defending herself.

"What is that moron's name?" I asked.

"Hedeon," she said.

"You're just inviting trouble for no reason," I said clasping my head.

"You will be in a restaurant filled with people, besides Bryan and me will be there too keeping an eye on you, so you don't have to worry," she said.

That actually sounded assuring.

"But this is the last date I'm going to." I said.

She squealed and jumped.

"Date's at seven," she said.

"I'm leaving at six," I told her making a face at her.

"Why so late?" She asked me.

"Overtime, extra pay." I told her making her laugh.

"What do you need so much money for?" She asked.

"I just sit at home and do nothing in the evenings." I stated.

"You need to relax and stop being a workaholic," she said checking her papers. "You should hang out with us and grab a drink sometime."

"I'll see," I said entering the strategies in my computer.

Melissa left at five.

"I'll pick a dress for you," she said ruffling my short hair before she went.

"Thank you," I said laughing.

I walked home at six after work. The day seemed a bit different. I had a feeling something unusual was about to happen.

I reached home about six-ten and saw that Melissa was already ready.

"Get ready," she said smiling and pushing me to the bedroom.

She had picked out a black dress for me which I had recently bought.

"This is so short," I complained.

"This reaches to past your knees. So it's not short. You'd look so pretty in it!" She said picking up the dress and showing it to me.

"I don't wanna go," I told her making a face.

"Stop making excuses! You're such a mood spoiler," she said handing me the dress.

"Fine mom!" I said rolling my eyes and walking to the huge walk-in closet to get dressed.

I stripped out of my dress and stood in front of the mirror looking at myself.

I had grown a bit on the chubby side. My face had grown chubbier than how it was when I had met him. My face was puffier and my full lips sat in a line a bit down my button nose. A pair of glasses sat on my nose, my eyes somewhat visible through the pair of glasses. I no longer had long hair. Instead a short pixie cut adorned my face. My fingers went up automatically to the scar on the right side of my forehead. A smile crept at the corner of my lips.

All I had with me was his memories and the scar...nothing else...

The images of the morning of our first date flashed across my eyes, in my mind.

I wonder where he is...how he looks...did he forget me and go for someone else?...

I gave out a sigh and put on the dress. The sleeveless dress showed off my collar bones and flaunted my figure, flowing down to my knees.

Was this guy worth it?

I grabbed on a pair of black and golden flats and walked out.

"You look so pretty!" Mel clapped and exclaimed.

I giggled and washed my face with a face wash and applied some moisturizer and brushed my teeth.

Even if I used to laugh, I was dead inside. I missed him a lot. Every time someone would bang at our apartment door, I would wish with all my heart that it would be him but then it would be someone else...

Every time I used to eat some berry, I would think of our first date.

Every time I would go for waxing or for a haircut, I would picture him laughing teasingly at me.

It was difficult for me to move on.

I was breathing in the fresh air after five years of prison but I still felt captive in my soul and only he had the key...

I wiped off my tears looking at myself in the mirror.

Even I had given up hope, but I still wished for him...

'This is not a goodbye,'

Why did you keep me waiting, Fyodor?

You could have just said that, that was a goodbye...and you could have saved me from so many tears and these years of prolonged pain...and this false hope ruining me...

I composed myself coming out of the bathroom.

Mel pulled out the chair for me to sit.

"Only some bb cream, powder and lipstick. I'm really in no mood for makeup," I said.

"As you wish, your majesty," she said making me laugh.

She did my base makeup and applied red lipstick to my lips.

"There you go. ta da!" She said.

"Thank you," I said hugging her tight.

"You know I'll be here for you," she said hugging me back.

I picked up my clutch and placed my glasses on my nose. We decided to walk to the restaurant as it was a five-minute walk.

"They have this super amazing sea food pasta which they recently put in their menu. Bryan says it's so good!" She said in her usual hyperactive chirpy voice.

"If you say so," I told her smiling.

I shivered a bit when we entered the restaurant. I was extremely nervous meeting this guy. The way Mel had described made him look so creepy to me.

Mel smiled and waved back when she saw Bryan waving at her. She ran to him and hugged him tightly. I saw him laughing and pecking her lips.

Couple goals and PDA as usual.

I shook my head and walked to them. As much as I hated to be the third wheel, I had no one else for support. I shook my head laughing and walking to them when they were talking.

Bryan gave me a friendly hug.

"Table seven," he said to me smiling.

"Thank you for placing the reservation," I smiled gratefully at him.

"Your date did all the arrangements," he laughed.

"Oh," I said walking down the rows of table unsure what or how to respond to that.

I was really not comfortable with male company and they both knew it. So they made sure that they were never offended when I made plain and blunt remarks to Bryan.

I went and sat at my table.

A few couples were enjoying the evening. Some were eating dinner while some were enjoying the evening over a glass of champagne. Ebony furniture was all over the place, fitted by maroon covers and tablecloths. The carpet was black and the entire place was lighted by soft lighting and candles which gave a seductive vibe to the place. Chandeliers adorned the ceilings. A choir of three singers played soft jazz music. Overall, the place seemed comfortable and warm, ideal for a date.

I saw a brown-haired man walk in the restaurant. I thought he was about to go to some other table when he came and sat in front of me.

I straightened myself up and that was when I remembered that I had forgotten to put any body fragrance on which made me, even more, self conscious than I already was.

"I'm Hedeon," he said in a voice which made the hair on my neck stand up.

My heart started beating abnormally faster.

It couldn't be...

I tried to observe his eyes which were well covered with glasses. The dim lighting in the room was making it more difficult for me to see.

"I'm Asha, you can call me Ash..." I said.

Looking closely at the guy, he had brown hair which was neatly combed. A five-o-clock shadow beard on his lower face. He even had a moustache. His facial skin was a bit rough but well hidden by his facial hair. He wore crisp faded yellow shirt concealed well with a long cloak and black tailored pants. A decent looking guy you could say.

He pulled out a bouquet of roses and placed it on the table in front of me along with a gift.

I placed my hand on the gift. It felt as if it had a dress in it.

It seemed that he had directly wrapped a glitter paper over a bundle of dress instead of putting in a box or anything.

I was normally used to receive flowers or small gifts like a key chain and stuff on dates.

He giving me such a kind of gift actually gave me a bad feeling in the pit of my stomach.

"Thank you, I guess..." I said in a low voice.

The time of day was perfect. The time between –after sunset and night– when the sky was not really dark. Shoppers passed by the window holding shopping bags while I was sitting inside a restaurant with a guy having a voice similar to that of some guy I had fallen for before.

I sat awkwardly for a while before picking up the menu and flipping through its pages while he did the same. But unlike me, he was actually going through it.

He was still going through the Menu when the waiter came and stood by our table. "I'm Jake and I'll be your server this evening. Your drinks and orders please?" He said smiling.

"I will have a beet salad with goat cheese as a starter, basil lemon crab linguine and for dessert, I'll have the strawberry cheesecake parfait," he said in a single breath.

"And for you, miss?" The waiter asked.

"Um...I'll just have what he ordered," I said.

"Any drinks?" He asked.

"I'll just have water," I said.

"Same here," Hedeon said.

I was still in a daze about the uncanny similarity he shared with Fyodor, the way he talked. It was so similar that it almost made me cry.

I saw the waiter walking away briskly folding his notepad and placing his pencil at the back of his ear.

I saw the waiter coming in and placing a glass each in front of us and pouring the water out of a jug and walking away again.

I had been on a few dates before, and as far as I knew, the other person and I would mainly indulge in talking unlike this case, where we were mostly focused on keeping quiet and eating.

It was as if someone was accompanying me as a dinner partner than being a date.

He looked quite unprepared. Often guys would try their best to look good. Their efforts would be quite noticeable, but with him, it seemed as if he came straight after work.

Unable to bear with the silence, I decided to start a conversation.

"So, how are you?" I asked.

"All fine," he said. "And you?"

"I'm good."

"You look pretty by the way."

"Thank you, but I have a question."

"Yes?"

"Why did you pay Bryan to go out on a date with me?" I blurted.

Where are my manners?

"I work with him at the laboratory, and I've seen you earlier. You came the other day to pick him up from work with his girlfriend. I found you attractive, so I asked him to introduce you to me. But he said you were not interested in anyone but I thought we should give it a shot. He was being very reluctant so I had to pay him and request him. Not that he has no money, I just wanted to show him how much this meant to me."

"Don't you think it's too much? I'm not even worth it."

He gulped and looked at me. I could swear his hands were balled into fists.

"Everyone deserves a chance."

I had no words for what he said.

I kept looking at my fingers on my lap when the waiter arrived with our food.

We started eating silently.

Only the clinking of the plate and cutlery was audible along with the soft music, the conversations of other people inaudible and oblivious to me.

I saw him finishing his pasta while I was just about to.

Wiping his mouth with a napkin, he said, "I really won't complain if you won't want to meet me again. I just thought you ought to have something you were not given a chance to own from a long time ago, even if it did belong to you."

He slapped our bill on the table, got up and left just like that. He did not even finish his dessert.

I felt really weird about what he said.

I looked at him as he excused himself and left in a hurry.

Unable to contain my curiosity, I opened the gift hurriedly to find a familiar looking green dress, under which was the familiar white dress with red flowers that I had worn on my first date. I ran my fingers across the inexpensive fabric of the green dress racking my brains hard to where I had got it from. I felt something hard beneath the softness of the clothes to find the same leather bound diary that I had once got nine years ago from the dirty wardrobe.

My throat fell dry. My heart was beating so fast that it threatened to skip out of my chest.

Fyodor...

It can't be him...

Mel came running to me followed by Bryan.

"Is everything alright?" She said rubbing my back.

I got up from my chair.

"Excuse me," I said. Picking up everything along with my phone, I ran outside the restaurant hoping him to be somewhere near.

I looked at the door of the restaurant only to find him gone.

I needed answers and only the brown haired guy could give me those.

I ran out panicked, hoping he might not be far.

I looked at either side of the pavement, but the man had vanished.

He could not have gone far.

I could see a brown head among the sea of people walking.

I ran towards him screaming, "Wait! Hedeon!"

I must have looked like a lunatic. Any lady wearing a fancy outfit and running around with two dresses and a barely wrapped leather diary clutched close to her chest would look like one.

Not to forget the purse.

I was actually surprised that I didn't drop anything.

I had just gotten closer to the guy when I discovered that he was wearing something else and that it was not him.

I had already gathered a few spectators who gave me weird looks.

I could not help but break down into a fit of sobs in the middle of a crowded pavement with people staring at me.

I felt a warm hand on my shoulder which startled me and there he stood, Hedeon.

My panicked and grief stricken face turned into one of normalcy when I saw him.

"Who are you and from where did you get this?" I asked him trying hard to fight back tears.

He held my wrist and walked into a narrow alleyway.

"STOP!" I yelled at him. The image of me pushing away Fyodor that day in the hallway flashed across in my mind.

He let go of my hand and looked down at me.

"Who are you and from where did you get this?" I demanded.

He leaned down to my ears and whispered, "You sure have some problem remembering me, darling."

My eyes shot open wide.

"You can't be Fyodor for sure," I said wiping the tears with my wrist.

Then he said the golden words of confirmation which I could have only imagined in my wildest dreams.

"It is me, Fyodor Vasiliev."

"Then how..." I asked looking at him top to bottom.

"The antidote, remember?" He said.

"It's too good to be true..." I said covering my mouth with my hands." I can't believe..."

"To a better future," he said leaning down to me, our foreheads almost touching.

I could not help but touch his face, his beard pricking my skin which hardly bothered me.

He smiled widely.

"Come, I'll show you," he said grabbing my wrist again and dragging me to his car which he had parked at a side of the road. He opened the door for me and asked me to get in. I saw him getting at the front seat in front of the steering.

Memories of the night we had spent last, nine years ago came fleeting back to me.

"I wish I could see your beautiful eyes," I said.

He laughed softly and removed his glasses and there they were. Two different colours, green and yellow and yet they made him look complete.

"I wish I could hug you though," he said making me grin.

I enveloped my arms around him in a tight hug. I felt his arms going around my back drowning me into warmth and comfort. I felt as if I belonged there.

My rightful place. Finally.

As uncomfortable our posture was, we still kept on hugging. We both were crying really hard but nothing mattered. We were yet to open a new chapter of our lives and nothing could come in our way now. We were clean and pure. We had learnt a lot. We were just another couple among so many others in this world but there were many things that made us stand out. Our experiences, the consequences that we dealt with; everything made us more powerful as an individual and as a couple together. I had given up the hope of all the positivity life had to offer but little had I known that I had to understand more about life. Love is so much more than fancy dates and having sex.

It is about caring for each other, being for each other no matter what, staying loyal to your partner, having the audacity to share your weak points with one another so that you heal each other and make yourself a better person. Love is about holding hands and walking together till you're old or alive, keeping your promises and elevating into a brighter future.

I had read once "Successful relationship means falling in love many times, always with the same person."

I had thought I would forget Fyodor, maybe move on but here he was, hugging me even after nine years of turmoil and separation, and that was enough for me to know that no man can be more perfect for me than him.

Fate is really strange.

Miracles will happen in your life if you have the courage to be on the right side.

"Hey..." He said softly into my ear.

I looked up at him.

"I know we never really got a chance to know each other but this much I know is that I can't really afford to lose you ever," he said with earnestness in his eyes. He pulled out a small box and opened it to reveal a pink diamond ring. "Will you do me the honour of being mine forever?" He said with glistening eyes.

This was a crazy path we were walking on. We did not even get time to catch up and talk about what happened after that night and yet here, he was proposing me.

These nine years had taught me that I could not live without him.

He was the water I had to drink.

The oxygen I had to breathe.

A drug I was addicted to.

"Are you sure?" I asked him raising an eyebrow.

"Does it look like I'm joking?" He asked.

"This is wonderful!" I said tearing up. "Yes!" I said and he slipped the ring on my ring finger.

I hugged him again sobbing really hard.

"Everything will be fine," he said stroking my head.

Hopefully, it will be.

Catching Up

After a while of hugging for long, he asked me if I wanted to crash at his place for the night to which I affirmed. He pulled his car out of the parking lot and started driving amongst the busy street. I just kept quiet and looked out of the window, the wind hitting my face. I could feel the wisps of hair brushing against my forehead as we sped against it. We left behind small, pretty coffee shops and a few stores as we sped forward. I smiled as I saw a Morphe store where I bought my makeup from. The number of cars seemed to have lessened down when he started speeding up. The road was clear. So was the road to our destiny.

I saw Fyodor turning on the car radio and as if on cue "Close to me" by Ellie Goulding started to play.

Even though we both knew we're liars and we ignited each other's fire

We just knew that we'll be alright.

Fyodor looked at me and smiled.

I smiled back and looked back outside while the song played. This was the perfect song for the moment. It was crazy how well I could relate to the song.

And I don't wanna be somebody without your body

Close to me

And if it weren't you, I wouldn't want anybody

Close to me

So true.

This was a beautiful moment. I felt the most beautiful than I had ever felt before. I felt like I belonged here, right beside him.

I used to shoo away people who would say that things would get better. I thought I was doomed. But now I know that things do get better; they always do if you're on the right side. And even if you went to the wrong side, you always have the chance to come back to the right side. You're always welcome to the better side. And you shall always be appreciated if you did so. Instead of rotting in the dark side being a bad person, it's always better to come to the light. You shall be accepted with open arms.

The drive was silent the entire time. I did not feel weird or uncomfortable; it was a comfortable silence.

I was mentally laughing at how he had transformed his taste in style, from that of a classy stud to a total nerd.

We must have driven for about twenty minutes when he pulled over under a head enclosure. There were several cars parked in a neat line.

"Here we come, to my house," he said smiling.

"Yay," I squealed excitedly like a little kid which made him laugh.

"You're crazy," he said getting out of the car, all smiles. He pulled open my side of the door.

I came out and kissed his cheek smiling, "Thanks for the compliment, gentleman."

I was sitting on the couch when he came and sat down near me placing two coffee mugs on the table. I looked at him as he scooted closer to me, pulling me over to him. Waves of nostalgia hit me hard while the events from nine years ago came flashing to me.

I buried my face into his chest, his smell...too overpowering... too overwhelming...I did not realize when I started breaking down into a fit of sobs.

"I thought I lost you..."

"I told you that was not the end," he cooed stroking my hair.

He gently lifted my head and kissed my forehead.

"I'm glad I surrendered...I'm living another life...and I don't regret it...thanks to you."

"It was all you...even if I would have tried to convince you a million times to do this, it was you who went for it," I looked into his beautiful eyes.

"I did not realize how much I loved you until I was away," he said tearing up.

"I missed you every second of the day," I whispered.

"So did I..."

"What happened after you were taken away though?" I asked looking at him curiously.

"Imprisoned, taken to court, I was given life sentence. I bet they would have given me death sentence if everything was revealed."

"What do you mean?"

"As for earlier records, the proofs related to other deaths were removed except for Edvin, Shandrel and Dasha, of course. So they gave me lifetime imprisonment for human trafficking and murder. But then per tests, they found out that I was mentally sick and unfit so they had me go for treatment. Hopefully, I changed and for my behaviour and improvement, they freed me. I'm living under a different identity...Hedeon Stalinski... also they were impressed with my work so...I carried on with my research with the government and here I am..." He said with occasional pauses. "What happened with you?..."

"They took me away back to India and had the cops interview me. They took me back to my home and then the rain of abuse started so I moved out. I was nearly dying on rail platforms when the child support found me and took me in, I finished high school and college, and worked in India for an NGO for a year and now I'm here for two years for work purpose, I work here for the educational department of children welfare committee."

"And your parents?" He asked seeming cautious.

"I really don't know; at first I heard they were arrested for abuse and then I voluntarily ignored them."

"You have me," he said rubbing my back.

"I did go to Russia though...to find stuff about you, a year ago... to Pegrema...but the property was sold and...I tried searching for you so bad but there was nothing I could lay my hands upon so I came back..."

He hugged me tightly. "I sold the property, yes...I bought a new one in Cornwall, England..." He said.

"What about the other people? Diana, Alyosha, Artyom..."

"Artyom didn't have a major hand in any of such things so he was released after five years, he and Alyosha have married and they're managing the property. Also Artyom is attending med school so life is getting back together," he said. "And the rest well...some are still stuck in legal procedures. I feel guilty about them sometimes..."

"I understand...changes do come with guilt..." I said.

I wiped my tears with my wrists.

"Hey...are you okay?..." He asked.

"I can't believe we pulled through this," I said, my voice cracking.

He kept playing with my hair while resting his head against mine.

"I can't believe I'm with you right now..." I said.

"I can't either...but this is the happiest day of my life, can't deny that."

"Can I ask you something crazy?" I asked.

"Mhm."

"Why do you love me? Or why did you even think about me that way..." I asked him.

"I don't know...you were so hell-bent on following the better aspect of life...facing it instead of running away like me...I couldn't help but get drawn to you...moreover when you didn't judge me and came forward to help me out...I knew you were my everything...someone I could come and talk to...someone who could teach me what is wrong and right...you, yourself made me fall for you...effortlessly...gracefully...how could have I let you go?..." He said sniffling trying to pull his tears back. "But most importantly I love you unconditionally...no reasons...just love...it's just my conscience which says I need you and in return, I'll be everything to you... And even if you turn into something bad...I'll not give up on you...promise..."

My thoughts went back to the second period during school days when the teacher had taught us "If thou must love me," by Elizabeth Barrett Browning...

If thou must love me, let it be for nought

Except for love's sake only...

I always had craved for those words but little did I know I would hear them one day and yet here, he was...saying them...

I looked into his eyes for a moment.

"I wonder how a person can be that perfect..." I said looking at him intently.

"Is it bad that the person wonders the same thing about you?" He said smiling a little before pulling me against his body and kissing me softly.

I closed my eyes and smiled like an idiot, my arms around his shoulder as our lips moved in sync with each other while my phone screen lit up with endless text messages from Melissa and the coffee mugs sat on the table, the steam fading away as the coffee got cold.

Intertwining Souls

Things started getting heated up really fast. I opened my eyes for a brief second to see his face drunk with an unseen passion which made my heart beat harder against my chest. He pulled away.

"What happened?" I asked him, almost disappointed.

"I'm not sure if you want this..." He said, his eyes piercing into mine.

"I do...I always have," I said.

"You sure?" He asked again.

I closed my eyes for a brief second taking a deep breath.

I grabbed his shirt and pulled him to me kissing him hard before climbing on his lap and straddling him.

"I hope that gives you my consent," I said joining our foreheads together.

I saw his cheeks redden, his pupils already dilated.

My lips travelled against his skin to his ears, "Now will you already take me in without further questioning." I whispered.

"No further questioning for sure," he said huskily, chuckling deep.

I could feel his warm tongue on my skin before he bit it gently, sending gentle tremors all through my body. I could hear him moan between his actions which turned me on even more. He was still sucking on my sweet spot as his hands travelled to my back like some mysterious creeper climbing on a tree before he unhooked my bra earning a gasp from me.

He looked at me giving out a naughty look as he unbuttoned and took his shirt off. I gulped looking at his well built and chiseled body.

"Nervous, dorogaya?" He asked pulling my body against his, my hands on his bare skin.

"Maybe a little…" I said, nervousness in my words.

"Hm…relax," he said sliding my dress and carefully removing it from the top of my head carelessly dumping my clothes across the table. I could feel his warm arms around me, my skin tingling as our naked skin touched.

I could feel his rough hands gently caressing my back as he kissed me again, his mouth devouring mine hungrily as I melted into him. I could sense his discomfort. It was difficult to guess if it was because of him getting hard or because of the size of the couch. I saw him taking off his glasses and mine as well. He pulled away tugging at my lip before he got up picking me up in the process and making his way to the bedroom and that was when he unleashed his carnal beast that had been deprived for so long.

I felt my back hit the soft mattress as he started trailing kisses from my lips to my chin and to my chest all the way down. I couldn't help but moan and that seemed to intensify and energise him even more. I could feel him grind against me causing me to clutch the sheets tight while my other hand was scratching his skin at the back as I threw back my head in a soft gasp. He came upon me and I saw his eyes for the last time that night as I never got a chance to reopen them that night, for my eyes had slid into pleasure and ecstasy throughout.

I felt his tongue perform wonders all over my body. And before I could do anything, he slid down his pants, tearing down my panties finally entering me. I wrapped my legs around his waist. I could hear and feel our wet skins slapping against each other as he held my hands above my head satisfying me to the core as I rotated my tongue around his earlobes, biting them gently, arousing him even more. The air was filled with grunting, moaning and creaking of the bed the entire time and that was how he made us one that night. I felt the most youthful I had ever felt, the most vibrant and the most zealous. I felt both of our flame torches, ignite and engulf our bodies and souls with a wildfire that we both had never felt before.

Two dancing flames are we,
Inseparable we are, yet we set each other free.
Lover thou art of mine,
Without thou, I can never be fine.
'Ignite me with your flare', say we to each other,
The world may say anything, we do not bother.

A Dream Come True

I looked at my finger, frail and wrinkly, but the wedding ring was still intact at its place shining as new as it was on my wedding day.

"Isn't it beautiful?" I asked Fyodor.

He laughed and wrapped his shaky hand around my shoulder. "It's beautiful if you think so," he said in a gruff voice coughing a bit.

I stroked his back and patted it slightly.

"Did you have your medicine this morning?" I asked him in a stern questioning voice, narrowing my eyes.

"I did."

"You're lying."

"No, I'm not!" He said defensively. "I did, I swear."

"Okay..." I said kissing his cheek, his wrinkly skin touching my lips.

I saw my grandson and granddaughter rolling their eyes at a distance looking at us.

"PDA! Eww!" Trisha said making a face. She really did take this PDA case too seriously. I smiled as my thoughts went back to the times of my younger days when I used to gag at couples exhibiting PDA.

We were sitting under a willow tree which overlooked the lake, watching our grandkids play. Thirty-nine years ago, I can still picture the entire place decorated with white flowers and ribbons as I walked on the path to a big gazebo at a distance at our left where we had exchanged our vows.

I smiled at Fyodor getting a smile from him in return.

I felt him entangling his fingers with mine, his frame shifting closer to me.

"This was one crazy lifetime," he said placing my hand within his.

I grinned looking at his shrunken eyes, but the colours evident. "It was. But it was all worth the effort."

"It was crazy," he said laughing.

"Yet I loved it," I said laughing as well.

"I wish I was young again," he said.

"Same here, but you know...we have to go one day, and the next generation will come in to have a chance of life."

"Death is a sad truth," he said looking down at my fingers.

I stroked his head running my fingers through his scalp, his hair still brown but with grey streaks. No matter how much I would tell him, he would always refuse to dye his hair. But then also, I did not care. We were together, and that is all that mattered.

"It is," I sighed. "But it's inevitable."

We rarely talked about death. It filled my heart with a deep sense of grief and sorrow. But then things which are supposed to happen will happen so I had decided to leave that to the moment when it would happen. So had he.

"I wonder how I ended up with such a beautiful angel."

I chuckled.

"I wonder the same."

He laughed, the distant excited squeals of the children echoing while we talked.

"Marry me in my next life as well," I said laughing. But we knew that within that laughter was a wish, a small whisper saying 'I wish it happens if incarnation and next life was true.'

"I always wish that we were together those nine years, and then maybe we could have spent those extra years together too."

I know I am fortunate enough to have gotten a chance to meet him again and have a life with him when there was hardly any chance of us getting together.

But it's human nature to remain unsatisfied no matter how much they have gained.

I'm a human after all...

"I will...and you know what? This is not over. I promise. I love you too much to let you go...be it any birth."

"I can't be sure or certain that this will happen.

We won't even remember each other.

What if we lose tracks and go for somebody else?"

"Do you trust me?" He asked me, squeezing my hand.

I broke out of my thoughts and looked at him.

"I do...I always have."

I knew I was giving myself more stress thinking about something I would never know anything about.

Focus on the present.

Forget about the past.

The future will be amazing.

Fate will work her way...

Promises

A young lady was standing in front of the grave of her grandmother. Despite the pouring rain, she still kept holding the black umbrella and kept looking at the grave intently. But her mind was quite not there. Her gaze shifted between the gates of the cemetery and the grave. She was waiting for her boyfriend who had said he would come so that they could pay their respects to her grandmother together.

She had already given up when she heard the bent metal gate creak. Her eyes lit up when she saw him running to her.

"Be careful! It's slippery!" She yelled as a warning.

He ran anyway engulfing her into a hug whispering the same thing he had always said,

"This is not over, I promise..."

She was expecting an apology or something else.

She gave a weird look as he always said those same words he used to whisper every time they hugged or when she feared about anything. As weird as that sounded, it felt comforting to her at the same time.

A sense of assurance...

A sense of relief...

"I trust you..."

She said as they hugged close while she kept on keeping the umbrella over their heads, protecting them from the heavy drizzle.

But no one watched the pair of heterochromic eyes looking through the girl's hair as he hugged her and the smile that he wore on his face.

He had won her...yet again...as always...